D1626878

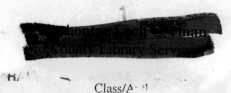
...hontae Leah Chapman
...County Library Service...

Class/A

THE HEART OF TEXAS

The war was over; the *Mississippi Belle* was
peacefully plying the river. But to two of 9
the passengers the scars of conflict were still
fresh, as were the scars of a personal conflict
pre-dating the national conflagration. Dan
Rather and John Marston had both loved
the same woman and had almost engaged in
a duel over her affections. Now Marston
was on his way to Texas to deliver a pardon
to a Southern officer whose daughter had
captured his deep interest. But when
Rather saw her picture he felt as if history
were repeating itself.

THE HEART OF TEXAS

Lynn Westland

ATLANTIC LARGE PRINT

Chivers Press, Bath, England.
Curley Publishing, 'Inc.,
South Yarmouth, Mass., USA.

Library of Congress Cataloging-in-Publication Data

Westland, Lynn, 1899–
  The heart of Texas / Lynn Westland.
    p. cm.—(Atlantic large print)
  ISBN 0–7927–1100–9 (pbk. : lg. print)
  1. Large type books. I. Title.
[PS3519.O712H4 1992]
813'.52—dc20   91–36722
                                                    CIP

British Library Cataloguing in Publication Data available

This Large Print edition is published by Chivers Press, England, and
Curley Publishing, Inc., U.S.A. 1992

Published by arrangement with Donald MacCampbell, Inc.

U.K. Hardback ISBN 0 7451 8353 0
U.K. Softback ISBN 0 7451 8365 4
U.S.A. Softback ISBN 0 7927 1100 9

© Copyright 1963 by Arcadia House

For Karoline and Oliver
In appreciation of many favors

THE HEART OF TEXAS

CHAPTER ONE

Evening had descended, the darkness hovering over the river like a hen above her chicks. In the dusk, the running lights of the *Mississippi Belle* appeared to float like a swarm of fireflies; the sound of the paddle wheel was muted. In that hush, the distant bark of a dog along the Louisiana shore was audible, the lowing of a cow. And from closer at hand, wafting across the decks, a quartette of voices, uniting on a popular favorite:

'—was a grand old man;
He washed his face in a frying pan,
He combed his hair with a wagon wheel
And died with a toothache in his heel—'

The man who had boarded the *Belle* that afternoon, registering as Berton Sebastian, abruptly stopped his pacing, drawing an involuntarily deeper breath of the soft air. Even in the gloom there was an aggressive set to his shoulders partially offset by the suggestion of a limp as he paced; that was the reminder of a Minie ball, whose aftermath of infection had been worse than the impact.

He was stirred not so much by the refrain as by certain of the words which reached his ear; other words and another name had been substituted, set to the popular tune, and he

1

had heard them often enough. The name of Old Dan Rather—

It might be only coincidence, that name and those words there aboard the *Belle*. No one could know him, under another name, a thousand miles from the country where he had campaigned during most of the years of war. And of course he was remembered, as was the parody—

Nonetheless, the song was disturbing, and it might be a warning. It paid to heed even small matters, when your life might be at stake.

Three courses were possible. He could vanish over the side in the gloom, making it to the shore without much trouble. But that would be wet and disagreeable, and the implied suggestion of flight was unwelcome. He could continue as Berton Sebastian, alertly watchful, giving no sign. Or he could meet the challenge head on, as he'd been accustomed to dealing with trouble in the past. Sometimes the most direct course was the safest.

The door of the saloon stood ajar, the soft light from hanging lamps flooding out, whitening the deck, touching the dark water at the side. The *Belle* had been newly repainted and refurbished at the war's end, and its appointments had pretty well succeeded in recapturing an era already fading into history. The voices issued from

2

that room; the door might have been left open intentionally.

He paused a moment in the doorway and, as always, he seemed to loom bigger than the five feet and ten inches of his height. Dark eyes searched from under bushy brows, considering the score of men who lounged indolently. Outwardly they were as select a company as the gentlemen who had frequented the *Belle* in days gone by. They walked and talked in measured cadences, impeccably courteous, though words might sharpen rather than sheath a barb. These were not the men of old; this was a company who had looked on damnation.

Aloof, watching with outward indifference, was Captain James Ordway—so his name was listed on the *Belle*'s roster. His eyes met Rather's without a flicker. What was John Marston doing there, under a false name? At the thought, Rather shrugged. The reason would probably be the same as his own, one in which their personal hatred played no part.

So it was unlikely that Marston had any connection with the song or with those who sang it. Old wounds had a way of continuing to ache, but blood, once spilled, was like water long run to the sea.

More likely some of the others had reason for the challenge, or believed they did. Some were ranged along the bar, while others played at dice with a languid air of studied indifference. A few were absorbed in the turn of a card, upon which fortune hinged. Schooling could mask a face but never quite hide the gleam in the eyes, with swift fortune or sudden ruin at stake.

One of the men lurched toward him, moving with timed deliberation. His face was flushed, and his words came somewhat slurred. The fellow was not quite drunk, but he was having trouble with his liquor—or cleverly using that as an excuse.

'Ha, gentlemen, here's luck!' he exclaimed. 'Here's a man might like to try his luck along with us. Perhaps you'd enjoy a cut of the cards, or a roll of the bones?'

'Why should I?' Dan asked indifferently.

'Why? Because Dan Rather has a reputation to live up to!'

Here it was, as blunt as his reaction to the song, which now he knew to have been deliberate. The fellow might be a Yankee; more likely, he was a renegade Southerner. Rather shrugged.

'Is that so, suh? I'm afraid you have the advantage of me. I don't know you.'

'That's easily remedied, Major. I'm McHugh—Joseph McHugh. And we have at least one thing in common. I, too, like a game for high stakes—the higher the better!' McHugh's glance was as coldly appraising as that of a professional buyer of human flesh.

Every eye was on them now, and Rather sensed danger. McHugh's words could well

4

hold a double meaning.

'What shall it be, Major Rather?' McHugh was blandly insistent. 'We like action here—nothing as long drawn out as a full game of cards. And a man can set his own stakes.'

He gestured toward the dice, to the other game where the turn of a card could spell ruin or fortune. It was all a pretext, of course. He had already played his big card by naming Dan Rather, getting him to admit to the identity. Since the name was as well known as the man, there was probably a respectable sum offered in bounty money. And McHugh intended to collect it.

Dan Rather smiled coldly. 'Since you know me, you should know that I seldom indulge in games,' he retorted. 'When I do, I like a flavor of excitement.'

McHugh was momentarily taken aback. The florid hue of his face altered like that of a chameleon.

'Excitement, did you say? What more can a man ask than this?'

The game was to be an instrument, no more than a pretext or the final act. It was true that these were plays that would bring riches or ruin. The strain showed on the flushed face of one man, gazing with triumphant avarice upon a diamond ring which he clutched. Under the light of the lamps, the stone was revealed as of surpassing value. It somewhat resembled a robin's egg, both in color and size.

A second man was in the background; he gazed with equal intensity at the ring, his breath coming in shallow gusts. Dan glanced at his hand; a circle on one finger was as whitely empty as the underside of a fish, while his cheeks matched in hue. His pallor told its story; he was an innocent already fleeced. The anger in Dan Rather grew. McHugh and the man who now clutched the ring had come aboard the *Belle* together.

'If you crave action, then there is a game which might interest you,' Dan suggested coolly. 'The officers of the Russian Czar sometimes indulge in it to alleviate the monotony of the long nights of winter. It consists in placing a loaded cartridge in a revolver, twirling the cylinder, cocking the gun, holding the muzzle to the temple and pressing the trigger. Each player has a turn.'

'I've heard of that game,' McHugh conceded. 'If that's the sort of thing you wish, I'm sure we can accommodate you, Mr. Rather.'

Dan observed how sharply John Marston was watching from the background. This was a ship of death. More than once, before the start of a battle, he had felt the same oppressive atmosphere.

'Sometimes there is no winner, therefore no loser,' Rather added softly. 'When there is a loser, the winner takes all.'

'Naturally.' McHugh's voice held a touch of impatience. 'It sounds to me like blind man's bluff. No man can guess in advance what he may be winning—if anything.'

'I have to disagree. I'd find it a waste of time even to play, without a stake upon the table.'

McHugh's new confidence wilted before his shrug. 'What do you suggest?' he asked.

'There's that ring,' Rather observed. 'Since the two of you are partners, you'll have no objection to putting it up?'

He caught the startled glance of the ring's late owner, the murderous glare in the eyes of the man who held it. McHugh hesitated, but he was caught and knew it. He resorted to bluff.

'Suppose I did arrange to put it up. You have something of matching value, perhaps? Or would we catch you in a bluff, Major Rather?'

'What I'll put up matches it,' Dan Rather said carelessly. 'But you'll have to take my word for it.'

This was a way out, and for a moment he thought McHugh was about to take it. Already the stakes were uncomfortably high for his taste. But he wet his lips and shrugged.

'Since your life is on the board, I'll risk your word,' he conceded. 'And now I

7

presume, since it's your suggestion, that you'll want to go first?'

Dan Rather's smile was mocking. As he turned his head, a small sliver of white hair showed amid the dark hair at the edge of his temple.

'The order is decided by the throw of the dice or the turn of the card. That adds to the interest.' He turned to the pale-faced man, whose finger bore the mark of the ring. 'Perhaps, suh, as a third party—you would favor us with the loan of your weapon?'

'The gentleman's name is Vanstyne,' McHugh volunteered.

Vanstyne nodded. A trace of color was creeping back to his face. He took a longbarreled Colt's from a coat pocket and tendered it with a bow.

'It is my pleasure, Major.'

'Thank you, Mr. Vanstyne. And of course you have a stake in this also, indirectly.' Rather broke the gun open, spilling the cartridges out onto the palm of his hand. He replaced one in the cylinder, then looked about with a cold smile.

'I think I should explain that I prefer a variation—shall we say an improvement?—on the Russian method. Where they have one loaded cartridge, I favor alternate loaded and empty chambers.'

Casually, he slipped two more shells back into the gun, with empty spaces between. No

8

one spoke. More than one face had paled, and McHugh's was ghastly. He opened his mouth as though to make some slighting remark, then, meeting the open mockery in Dan Rather's eyes, left the words unsaid. The tune and words of the parody rang in men's ears:

'He combed his hair with a wagon
        wheel—'

Here was the man in the flesh, a giant in reality and by tradition. The name Dan Rather was a synonym for recklessness.

'Of course,' Rather added with a shrug, 'the empty shells are left in the gun through successive turns, and the cylinder is spun each time.'

'Turns? My God!' There was no longer any question that McHugh had gotten more than he had bargained for. 'I'm not ready to commit suicide,' he blurted. 'I find life too interesting to throw it away for nothing. The bets are off.'

Turning abruptly, he plunged from the room, and his confederate, still clutching the ring, was at his heels. Rather looked about, to return the gun, and found its owner also among the departed. Some of the men who remained congratulated him, speaking warmly. As soon as he could, Rather left as well, returning the rest of the loaded cartridges to the gun. It might be the part of prudence to replace it with his own weapon, he decided, looking about for Vanstyne but failing to see him.

His counter-move had balked McHugh, but it would mean only a delay in the game. McHugh was the type who would cherish a grudge, and his original purpose would remain unaltered. His scheme had backfired, but there were other ways.

Dan Rather had returned to the rail, and was staring pensively over the side, watching the swimming moon, when he heard a splash. It was not loud—the sound was almost covered by the churning of the big paddle wheel—but like his eyesight, Dan Rather's hearing was acute.

He swung, searching the river's surface, then was over the side in a long dive, even as his shout rang out.

He went under, then fought back to the surface, away from the froth of the churning wheel, with its insidious pull. The weight about his middle was a heavier impediment than he had counted on, but he swam strongly. Presently he saw what he sought, and a moment later the pasty-faced man with the desperate eyes struggled frantically in his grasp, panic of a new sort having him in its grip. He had been about to go down for the third time, and even to those who leap to meet death, its embrace may be unpleasantly chill.

The sound of voices, along with a change in the throb of the engines, reached Dan

Rather's ears. Someone had heard his shout, had looked in time to see him jump. The *Belle* was slowing, starting to drift back with the current. He spoke commandingly, reassuringly, and the panic faded in the eyes gazing up at him, the desperate flailing arms relaxed.

'Catch it!' A rope came sailing, flung out acoss the water as the packet veered. Dan lifted an arm and clutched it, then worked desperately to cast it aside. It was not a length of rope, but a loose coil, settling over and about them. There was no end still held aboard the boat, but there was something else—some heavy weight, hastily attached, which would drag and hold them down if the coil managed to entangle them.

CHAPTER TWO

The ruse almost worked. A spreading coil of rope, with a weight attached, could be like the arms of Medusa.

Dan Rather kept his head and worked free, allowing the rope to sink without them. Then willing hands were alongside, reaching, pulling them aboard.

'Why didn't you let me go?' Despair was in Vanstyne's voice. He had not even understood about the rope. 'I'm ruined. You

11

suggested a way out. Now I won't have the nerve to make a second try.'

'No need for that,' Dan said reassuringly. 'We'll find the gentleman—and I'm sure he'll be happy to return your ring. After all, such practices are not allowed aboard a boat such as the *Belle*.'

'I should have known better than to wager it. But I'd been winning—'

'That is the usual way. Think no more about it.'

Everyone was crowding around, excited by a man overboard. McHugh's friend was not among them, and a word to Captain Hanning brought no better result. He called an assembly in the main saloon, then ordered a search of the ship. Lamont had apparently availed himself of the confusion to go over the side as well. He, too, would be confident of making the shore.

The search had the effect of restoring Vanstyne's morale. He expressed his thanks effusively.

'The ring was an heirloom, and when I lost it, I guess I lost my head as well. It's not irreplaceable, or something I can't live without, though for the moment I felt that way. I'm grateful to you for saving me. Words, of course, are a feeble show of gratitude—'

Dan Rather escaped further thanks by suggesting that both of them would be the better for dry clothing. Vanstyne acceded, and they returned, each to his own cabin. As he stripped off his wet garments, Dan pondered the changed atmosphere aboard the *Belle* since the days before the war.

In those days, Captain Hanning, like his craft, had been a synonym for integrity. But a man, like conditions, could change.

He had finished arranging the wet clothing over the back of a chair to dry when something surged against his door and jarred it open, crashing inward. A huddle of figures in fierce conflict spilled through, and the rays of the moon flashed on a knife blade. Since it was at least two to one, and the attack so murderous, Dan Rather moved into the fray on the side of the underdog.

It was too dark to see much, for his own candle puffed out in the draft made by the opened door. Instinct availed as much as eyesight, and he knew that it was Colonel John Marston who, having collided violently with the door, then staggered through, was going down. He sprawled on the floor, and the knife wielder leaped for him.

Dan smashed with the open flat of his hand, and luck was in the stroke as well as skill. It spun the assailant to his knees, sending the knife clattering along the floor. He sensed the second man was swinging at him and lifted his foot, kicking out with his back to the wall. That stroke too was nicely timed. It drove the breath from the other man, even as it hurled him back through the door, to sprawl and roll along the deck, before he got to his feet and scuttled away.

Finding himself weaponless, suddenly alone in the fray, the first man followed. Definite recognition was impossible under the conditions, but Dan's guess was that McHugh had once more proved he had no liking for a fight where the odds were not stacked in his favor.

The surprising thing was that this assault had been directed against Marston rather than himself. Dan closed the door and relighted his candle. Its light showed Marston, still doubled on the floor, breathing but senseless.

Ordway's face showed pale in the light of the candle, but it had lost none of its good looks in the last half dozen years. He was Dan's senior by several years, though he looked no older. Both of them had fought gallantly for the South. This present trouble might well have its roots in those war years.

Their hatred was even older, antedating the war. A women had been the cause, the motivating force. They had both loved her. And, giving justice where it was due, John Marston had not known about Dan Rather when he had first fallen hopelessly in love with her.

Later, upon learning that she was pledged to Rather, he'd come to Dan offering

14

satisfaction with small swords or pistols at ten paces; an offer which Dan Rather had declined, somewhat to his own as well as to Marston's amazement.

'Since she prefers you, as she assures me is the case, why should I kill you?' Rather had demanded. 'Then she'd have nothing left, for I wash my hands of her. As for shooting men, there are Yankees enough to occupy both of us.'

The denial of satisfaction, the implication that he would kill Marston, had been an affront to the colonel's pride, never forgiven. His own sense of loss and injustice had lingered, though he had learned later that she had died within the year. Even the memory of the past now left him cold and empty.

He bent above Ordway, wondering if he should get water or call for help, yet reasonably sure that he would revive in good time. Then his breath caught. A packet of papers had fallen from Ordway's pocket, partially opening, spilling across the floor. Stooping, he met the eyes of a woman—a face in a photograph which seemed to look directly into his. Nor was this an ordinary picture of any ordinary woman.

It had been a long while, more than half a decade, since any woman or her likeness had been able to quicken his pulse, but here was one with the power to do so. Ironically, it appeared that Ordway also knew this woman.

She had a girl's face, with wide-open eyes, a heart-shaped, strongly appealing countenance. The picture was not a tintype, but a photograph in the latest tradition, one to match the best work of Matthew B. Brady. Brady, during the course of the war, had raised the art of picture making to new levels.

Dan judged her to be a year or so beyond twenty, slight yet strong. She was bare-headed and full-lipped, with a hint both of challenge and promise in her level gaze.

The eyes seemed to meet his own, half laughing, half serious. Dan picked up the photo and studied it more closely, impelled by a feeling that here was destiny. He saw an inscription written across one corner, a personal message:

'*With all my love. Texas.*'

Dan sighed. The words were not for him; he felt a rekindling of the old animosity at the realization that they had been intended for Marston. The luck of the man! The unwarranted fortune, that two such women should both prefer him—

There was something else. He picked it up, not intending to look closer. But the sheet, folded but now spread partly open, was of heavier than ordinary parchment, the handwriting firm but somewhat scrawling. The signature at the bottom seemed to leap out from the page:

'A. Lincoln.'

Abraham Lincoln! The man who, despite himself, he had come to respect, then to admire, finally almost to love. Lincoln was long months in his grave, and the tragedy of his assassination was the tragedy not only of the South, but of the nations; of men like himself, whose fate might have been far different had Lincoln lived.

Deliberately, lips tightening, he read the missive. It was straight-forward and simple, explicit. A pardon, in the President's own handwriting. A full, unconditional pardon for Randolph Minifee, sometime General in the Armies of the Confederacy.

Minifee! The name was almost as familiar as his own. If his exploits had caused men to parody a song, the name and reputation of Randolph Minifee had spread as far. On one occasion Minifee, his forces frustrated and held in check at every turn, had boldly donned the uniform of a captured Union officer, then had taken that gentleman's place for a full week, beyond the Union lines. Granted that it had been a period of battle and much confusion, and that the officer had been temporarily despatched to serve among men strange to him (as Minifee had discovered), still it had been a reckless gamble. At the slightest slip, he could have been promptly placed in front of a firing squad as a spy.

Minifee had carried it off; in the process,

giving conflicting orders, he had badly disrupted the whole Yankee war machine in those parts. He had staved off imminent defeat for his comrades; more importantly, he had made monkeys of important men, who were inclined to be unforgiving.

There had been other feats, and Dan had heard that Minifee's name, like his own, was on the proscribed list. Beyond doubt he was being sought. If captured, he could expect a spy's death.

And John Marston carried a pardon for him! The reason for the murderous assault was clear enough.

Thoughtfully, Dan replaced the pardon and the photograph in the envelope, again studying the letter. Then he saw that Marston's eyes had opened and fixed upon him.

'These spilled on the floor,' Dan explained, and tendered the envelope.

Marston sat up, shaking his head uncertainly. He accepted the envelope and replaced it in an inner pocket, eyes roving the room. 'You saw?' he asked.

Dan nodded. 'The pardon? Yes. It was open, on the floor—and when my eye caught the signature, A. Lincoln—I'll confess I was curious enough, and ungentlemanly enough, to read it.'

'A quite natural curiosity and one, under the circumstances, which was quite justified,'

18

Marston protested. He struggled to his feet and, with Dan's assistance, to a chair. 'I take it that this is your room, and that I owe my life to you. That pair took me by surprise.'

'They seemed intent upon doing you in,' Dan murmured.

'I'm afraid they might have succeeded.' He stooped and picked up the fallen knife, a bowie. Its edge had been whetted to a razor keenness. 'The weapons of treachery,' he added dryly.

'Exactly. You were driven against the door, which burst open, and apparently knocked you out at the same time.'

'So I find myself indebted to you. Naturally, I'm grateful—though I find it somewhat embarrassing.'

'You recognized them? We should report this to the captain.'

'They wore masks,' Ordway said evasively, 'handkerchiefs over their faces. Also, it was rather dark.'

'As you will. But you run a grave risk while they remain on the loose.'

'Perhaps. On the other hand, I've grown accustomed to that sort of thing. Fortunately, because of you, they failed in their objective—which, of course, was this pardon.'

'It would seem reason enough.'

'To them, certainly. Some of us—I, for one—was foolish enough, for a while, to believe that the war was over. We fought for a principle. Perhaps we were wrong. In any case, it no longer makes much difference. We lost. I was willing to let bygones be bygones, to start over. I think we were all heartily sick of slaughter. And some high and pious platitudes were proclaimed—'

Dan nodded understandingly. He, too, had hoped for peace, but it had turned out to be a false dawn. The brief sun of peace had risen, only to fall back in bloody disarray with the shooting of Abraham Lincoln. Lincoln had meant what he had said about binding up the wounds of war. But there were many others who did not want that.

Now, with Lincoln dead and his successor rendered largely impotent, such men occupied the seats of power. They had an appetite for vengeance, and their reach was long. Amnesty had been granted the foot soldiers, but now, almost a year later, a price was being put upon the heads of many, such as Minifee, Marston and himself. That, of course, was why John Marston went by the name of Ordway, why Dan had come aboard as Berton Sebastian—precautions which had proven futile.

'Perhaps you noticed the photo I carry—the picture of Texas Minifee?' Ordway asked, with seeming carelessness.

'I saw that you had a picture.'

'Then you'll perhaps agree that she's worth

taking a few risks for,' Ordway suggested. 'She's the daughter of General Minifee. I became acquainted with her when, during the height of the late struggle, this remarkable woman managed to visit her father in his camp. It was no light matter, in such troublous times, to journey from a ranch in the heart of Texas, across a land ravaged by war, to perform so filial an act. Her presence, even for a few brief weeks, greatly cheered her father and inspired others. Afterward she returned to her home, the great Randolph Ranch, founded by the general some two decades ago and located, I understand, on the Colorado.

'I was acting as an aid to General Minifee during the course of her visit, so had the pleasure of making her acquaintance. Later, naturally, she turned to me for assistance in a moment of dire trouble. After hostilities ended, the general made his way back to Texas to his ranch—hoping to resume life, as nearly as possible, where it had been interrupted half a decade before.'

Dan nodded his understanding.

'The general was fortunate in being able to return to so remote a country, since the hunt for him was already under way. Since then, it has intensified. I understand that he remains secluded, though not to the degree the situation calls for, or which his friends and his daughter would prefer. But you know his reputation, sir. He is a reckless man, who delights in taking chances.'

Dan could understand. His own byplay with the three loads in the revolver came under a similar heading. Actually, such calculated risks were far less dangerous than hesitation in the face of danger.

'Miss Texas requested of me a favor, which she admitted might be difficult. But for her sake, as well as the general's, I undertook it, journeying to Washington—again as James Ordway. Luck was with me. I realized that such an appeal as I had to make, if directed to any source such as the Secretary of War, would be spurned. No one short of President Lincoln could or would grant what I sought. By then, events had confirmed my growing belief that Abraham Lincoln was a great-hearted man; a man much misunderstood, but a true friend of the South—since it, in his eyes, remained a part of the Union.'

Dan inclined his head. 'I agree.'

'As I say, luck was with me. I was takin' a walk in the dusk of evenin', strollin' near the capital. I encountered the President himself, also enjoyin' the night air. I had the temerity to accost him and identify myself. From that I proceeded, with his permission, to tell him what I wanted—a pardon for my friend. I showed him the letter from Texas—Miss Texas—a most appealin' letter, suh, which affected him as it had me.

'The upshot, suh, was that he wrote out the pardon for General Minifee, in his own handwritin', signed it and gave it to me. He remarked as he did so that some of his advisers, such gentlemen as Mr. Stanton, would disapprove very strongly. But the war was over, and he was concerned with binding up the wounds of a nation, not with further unnecessary blood-lettin'. He also gave me an excellent piece of advice: to hold fast to the pardon, until I could deliver it into the hands either of the general or of Miss Texas herself. This I have endeavored to do—and successfully, with your timely aid tonight. Otherwise, the President assured me, attempts might be made to destroy it. He spoke prophetically.'

Dan nodded again. He had seen and heard enough in recent weeks to attest to Abraham Lincoln's wisdom. Unless a pardon was presented at the proper time and place, it could be rendered ineffective by any one of several methods.

'During a period of months,' Marston went on, 'I have done more skulking and hiding than I ever found necessary before. Despite several hindrances, I have succeeded in getting this far toward Texas. I hope to arrive in time—but time becomes vital for the general and Miss Texas. It would break her tender heart should her pappy be shot as a

23

spy at this late date.'

He stood up unsteadily.

'So my thanks to you are double, suh—and if you suffer any embarrassment at having helped me, then consider that it was a service rendered to General Minifee and Miss Texas. I shall tell them of the assistance you have rendered. Good evening, suh.'

CHAPTER THREE

Dan wandered astern, while the *Mississippi Belle* continued to churn against the current. Most captains would have pulled over to a bank and tied up for the night, but Captain Hanning had no intention of doing so as long as silver flooded the river.

He turned his head at a step. Captain Hanning was beside him, glancing to where the lights of a farmhouse made a pin-prick against the dark line of the shore. A rooster, perhaps disturbed by the packet's running lights, crowed; the sound was remote and lonesome.

'A beautiful evening,' Hanning murmured. Dan assented, and for a while they watched in silence. Dan waited for him to mention the disturbance in his cabin, but apparently he was not going to bring it up. Yet it seemed strange that the commotion could have passed unnoticed. Then Hanning spoke again, and his words seemed oblique.

'Is it wise for you to go unarmed, Major—after what has already happened?' he asked.

'Unarmed?' Dan repeated. 'But I always go armed.'

Hanning's sigh sounded relieved. 'I was noting the absence of your revolver, which usually bulges your coat pocket,' he explained. 'Your game of triple Russian roulette won you a measure of respect—but not of affection!'

'Oh, that?' Dan's smile froze as his fingers felt instinctively for his weapon. It was not in its accustomed place.

'You're right,' he acknowledged. 'I hadn't noticed its absence. I must be growing careless.'

'Some men are deft at lifting a purse or a gun,' Hanning observed. 'In your case, it could be meaningful.'

'It's a piece of carelessness I can't afford,' Dan admitted ruefully. 'And there are some strange characters aboard, Captain.'

Hanning's sigh seemed rueful.

'Before the war, our passenger list was selective. The *Belle* was intended as an accommodation for gentlemen—and ladies, of course. Now—anyone who has the price of a ticket can come aboard.'

Dan's reply was interrupted by the sharp

bark of a gun. The sound was muffled by the noises of the boat, but was still distinct and ominous. An instant later, Hanning was running, Dan at his heels.

At their approach, a shadowy figure darted from the deeper gloom of an open doorway and fled. Dan gave chase, but in the darkness it was impossible to follow. He turned back, following Hanning into the cabin.

The room was a pool of darkness. Hanning was fumbling to get a light. He succeeded at that moment, and both of them saw Marston, sprawled on his back in the middle of the floor. Close above the heart, the colonel's white shirt was smudged and torn, as from the burn of powder and lead. Curiously, there was no blood.

The captain bent over him for a quick examination. He arose, turning to close the door, and his face was grave.

'I'm afraid we're too late,' he said.

Footsteps sounded outside; others had been attracted by the sound of the shot. Hanning went to the door to confer with them, momentarily closing it behind him. Dan stared down at the motionless figure on the floor, a prey to mixed emotions.

The second attack, following so swiftly on the heels of the first, apparently had taken Marston off guard. Two of the five buttons of his coat had been loosened. Dan bent down, thrusting a hand inside, and drew it out with a sigh of relief. Apparently their prompt arrival had frightened away the killer an instant short of achieving his objective. A quick check showed that the pardon and the photograph were intact. Dan hesitated, then, as the door started to open, thrust the envelope into his own pocket.

Captain Hanning lingered a moment in the open doorway. By now, several men were congregated outside.

'There's been a shooting and possible robbery,' he explained. 'Major Rather and I will conduct an investigation. The rest of you may go back to your rooms, but not to bed. I'll be making a check soon.'

Calling certain members of the crew, he took charge, shutting all others from the cabin. Later, everyone was assembled in the main saloon.

With the exception of Lamont, who apparently had gone overside before, no one was missing. Hanning explained what had happened bluntly and with no waste of words.

'We've had a killing and apparently a robbery. Some man or men forced their way into Captain Ordway's cabin and shot him. This hearing will be continued in the morning, when I intend to get to the bottom of this.'

As captain, aboard his own boat, he could handle things according to his own notions.

He ordered the packet to put in and tie to a convenient tree. Should anyone take advantage of the proximity to shore to decamp during the night, he could expect to have the law set upon his trail.

As anticipated, no one made a foolish move. With the first rays of dawn, there was a stirring on board, and a crew of workmen was sent ashore. They dug a grave on a green slope back from the river, then carried ashore a hastily built coffin. Hanning requested everyone to assemble for the funeral.

'We can do no less, for so gallant a gentleman, than show him a last proper respect,' he pointed out. The sun was bright and birds were singing as he intoned ancient, everlasting words, while heads were bowed. Once that was done, there were murmurs of surprise as the captain gave orders to return on board for the completion of the run to St. Louis.

'You mean this is all?' McHugh demanded. 'We just bury him and then go on?'

'The *Belle* has a schedule to follow. I keep to it as closely as circumstances allow.'

McHugh stepped to the foot of the grave, turned and faced the group with an uplifted hand.

'Before we go on, Captain, may I inquire what else you propose to do to discover the murderer of this gentleman?'

Hanning nodded. 'You may. Once we

reach St. Louis, I shall make a full report and turn the matter over to the proper authorities.'

'Is that all?'

'What else is there?' Hanning asked irritably. 'It is the legal and accepted procedure in such cases.'

'And the authorities, as you call them, will prate piously, as has already been done over this poor fellow, and nothing more will come of it,' McHugh retorted. 'I object to such methods. You promised that a full inquiry would be made this morning, and I feel that it should be—here and now.'

'You are implying that one has not been conducted?'

'Let me say that the whole procedure to date strikes many of us as superficial. If anything is to be learned concerning this unfortunate affair, is not this the time and place?'

Captain Hanning's jaw thrust forward pugnaciously. 'Are you accusing me of shielding a murderer, sir?' he demanded.

'I make an observation, not an accusation,' McHugh returned silkily.

'Very well. Just what is it that you think has been omitted which might have been done?'

'Quite a bit, Captain. Some of us have been making inquiries, for our own information. For one thing, the presence of everyone on

29

board at the time of the shooting seems to be accounted for, with the exception of the man who was found first in Captain Ordway's room, immediately following the latter's untimely demise.'

At that charge, every eye swung to Dan Rather. Hanning grunted.

'Is such conjecture all that you have to present?' he demanded.

McHugh smiled and shook his head. He reached into a pocket and pulled out a gun, holding it up to view.

'I'm wondering if we might not identify this gun and its owner,' he said. 'I repeat that the search, following the shooting, was superficial, and I offer this as proof. Looking around there soon afterward, I stumbled across this, not far from the door of the murdered man's cabin. Apparently it had been hastily tossed away, probably intended to go over the side and into the river. But it must have hit the railing and fallen back, unnoticed. One shot had been fired—very recently fired, since the smell of burnt powder still lingered when I picked it up.'

The sympathy of most of the passengers had been with Dan Rather up to that point. Now there was an uncertain murmur.

'It is common knowledge that Major Rather was first on the scene—ahead of everyone else. And if you will examine this weapon, Captain, you will observe initials carefully etched in the metal—the initials D.R.'

Hanning accepted the gun, examined it, and looked expectantly at Dan.

'Is this your missing gun, Mr. Rather?' he asked.

Dan nodded. 'It is.'

'Have you finished, Mr. McHugh?' Hanning went on.

McHugh shrugged. 'It seems to me that the evidence speaks for itself.'

'Why, now, you may be right. I fancied that you'd come forward with something of the sort, if the occasion seemed to warrant. I might question your tale about how you came into possession of this weapon, Mr. McHugh, or why you were so dilatory in turning it over to me. But of course you made certain that there were no witnesses.'

McHugh bridled. 'Are you implying, Captain, that *I* had anything to do with this matter—other than what I've just told you?'

'You had a grudge against Major Rather,' Hanning reminded. 'And I will say for all to hear that I do not believe your story. As to this gun and its owner, I will say this: Major Rather and I were standing together, in the after part of the boat, when we heard the shot. We ran together and reached the cabin at the same time.'

McHugh's face suddenly lost its color. Hanning shrugged.

'Under the circumstances, I am sure that the authorities at St. Louis will be interested in your story, sir. I shall make certain that they hear it.'

Everyone returned on board, the *Belle* cast off, and now the atmosphere was tense. The manner in which McHugh had been caught in his own snare was not lost on the others.

They tied up in St. Louis late in the afternoon, and there, true to McHugh's prediction, the turning over of the affair to the authorities buried it as deep as the coffin on the little hillside. McHugh was sharply questioned, but since there were no eye-witnesses, no one was detained. His story of finding the gun furnished no grounds for holding him on a more serious charge. The formalities were observed, which was all that anyone had expected.

Troubled by the lack of firm steps toward justice, Dan Rather took such precautions as seemed expedient, losing himself in a crowd, once he had merged with the homeward flow of carriages and pedestrians. He doubled and twisted until he was confident that anyone who might have sought to keep him in sight would have been frustrated. Thereafter he chose a small hotel on a back street and secured a room, before going out for supper.

It was dark when he returned; his plans were reasonably well formulated. Until a couple of days before, his intention had been to lose himself along the frontier, with no particular destination in mind.

Now his way was chosen. He'd take a stagecoach west. He'd have to cross Missouri and a corner of The Nations before he could reach Texas; and once the Lone Star State was attained, he would be in the midst of a vast sprawling country which was still largely wilderness. Deep inside Texas lay the Randolph Ranch.

Inquiries had already made clear that stages ran only a part of the way across Missouri. After that, where settlements thinned, there was no regular means of transportation, often none beyond what a man might secure for himself. The border country wallowed in poverty, rendering commercial ventures extremely hazardous. Besides, the border was beyond even the shadowy protection of the law.

He had let himself into his room before he sensed that it was already occupied. By that time a clubbed weapon was chopping viciously from behind the door, and Dan Rather staggered and went down in red-shot, blinding darkness.

CHAPTER FOUR

Dan Rather fought back to consciousness, as a sinking swimmer struggles to regain the surface.

He opened his eyes barely enough to see, conscious of a blinding light which beat against the eyeballs and sent waves of agony coursing in his skull. He again closed his eyes.

Gradually the pain eased, and his mind began to function again. He was sprawled on the floor, lying partly doubled and on his left side, as he must have dropped when slugged. The light was that of a candle, guttering jerkily. Normally it would have appeared weak and small against the darkness, but pain imbued it with monstrous qualities.

Having sorted out the obvious facts, he opened his eyes again, making no other move. It required a minute of study, but by then he had the picture. Two men were in the room, and one was McHugh. The other was Lamont, which he did not find particularly surprising. He'd guessed all along that the fellow was being concealed somewhere aboard the *Belle*, probably on account of Vanstyne's diamond ring, so that its return could not be forced. He'd have made his way ashore in the confusion of unloading.

34

And Lamont could easily have wielded the knife, and later used the gun against John Marston—unless McHugh had done the job himself.

Regretfully Dan admitted that he hadn't given them proper credit for shrewdness and tenacity. They had managed to keep him in sight and see where he had secured a room, keeping so far back that he'd been unaware of them. Once he had gone out, they had entered and waited. In that part of town, that had not been hard to manage.

Having knocked him out, they had wasted no time before searching him. He knew what they sought. Not that they were adverse to extra windfalls, and they had come upon one. They had found his money belt and unbuckled it from about his waist. Now, forgetful of all else, they were pouring out handfuls of gold coins, running the eagles through the fingers, gloating at the richness of their find.

Such naked greed was a mistake. Not only did it render them incautious, but that money had been hard come by, over a period of years, and Dan Rather had no intention of permitting it to be taken. Though his head still throbbed, it was clearing to a bearable degree. He moved his right hand carefully, his fingers closing on the fat stock of a derringer. He had long been in agreement with Captain Hanning that it was unwise to be without a weapon.

As he twisted to a sitting posture some small object scraped under his foot. McHugh turned fast.

That was a mistake, as was the carpetbagger's grab for his own gun. The crash of the derringer was shockingly loud in the confines of the room, and the candle flame flickered and wavered in the concussion, but continued to burn. McHugh, his revolver half-drawn, recoiled in shock; his gun arm dropped, blood making a sudden stain along the sleeve below the elbow.

Lamont turned more slowly, in time to see the mist of smoke which puffed from the muzzle. Fright washed over his face, and he backed until halted by the wall, arms raised jerkily.

Dan got slowly to his feet steadying himself against the rocking sensation of the room. Silence succeeded the roar of the gun, a hush out of all proportion to the situation. All normal noises seemed to have been stilled, leaving no others to take their place. He smiled grimly, for the night clerk and others in the hostelry should have been rushing out to investigate the disturbance. The fact that no one was doing so spoke volumes.

He reached with his free hand, finding the knob and wrenching open the door, and raised his voice in a shout.

Lamont cringed and made as if to protest,

36

but thought better of it and waited. Presently, in answer to the call, the clerk came, a pale-faced man creeping slowly up the stairs, his head moving from side to side like a fox testing the air. He carried a lantern which gave a fuzzy light. He moved uncertainly, ready to take to his heels at the slightest excuse, but he came.

'Did—someone call?' he quavered. 'I thought I heard something.'

'You must have heard plenty, unless your ears are for purely ornamental purposes,' Rather told him. 'Call a constable, or any law officer. I caught these fellows in my room, trying to rob me. You must have a marshal or policeman somewhere in the town,' he added impatiently, as the clerk gawked doubtfully from the gloom of the hallway.

'Well—yes, yes of course. There should be someone—'

'Then find him, and fast. Or am I to suppose that you're allied with thieves at work in your own building?'

That brought a response, perhaps because the accusation hit home and might coincide with suspicions already entertained by such law as the city boasted. The clerk scurried back down the stairs, trailing voluble promises. Lamont took a venture at persuasion.

'Do you think this is wise?'

Dan stifled the natural retort. It was often

useful to probe another man's thinking, especially an enemy's.

'You can advance reasons, perhaps, as to why it might not be?'

Lamont shrugged and nodded and started to lower his arms. At the gesture of the derringer he hastily elevated them again.

'Need I remind you that one man has died for interfering in the wrong affair? Perhaps that was his business but it can't reasonably be yours. So it might be wiser to forget what is no concern of yours.'

'I could quite reasonably put a bullet through your head or your heart—giving you the benefit of the doubt and assuming that you possess a heart,' Dan returned. 'I would be entirely within my rights. Perhaps I should follow your advice and do so.'

Meeting the glint in Rather's eyes, which in the reflected light of the candle matched the flicker along the steel gun barrel, Lamont lost color and fell silent. He made a tentative move to the side, and stopped at the sharpness in Dan's voice.

'Back where you were! Try to puff out that candle and you'll blow out your own brains.'

Lamont returned hastily to his former position, shivering. His eyes held grudging respect. Those songs and stories about Old Dan Rather appeared to have some foundation.

McHugh was clasping his injured arm with

his other hand, leaning against the wall. The shock of the heavy-caliber bullet was beginning to take effect, and Dan knew that for the time being he had nothing to fear from McHugh.

Apparently the clerk had not had far to go. Heavier boots tramped up the stairs; then a short, thick-set man appeared, his bulbous nose giving an illusion of lighting his way. But in the next few minutes he went far toward redeeming the soiled reputation of the city.

'You are the man who sent for me?' he asked. 'And these are the men who tried to rob you?'

Dan nodded. 'They were waiting when I entered my room. They slugged me, and had my money belt off when I came to and got the drop on them. They were too busy with it to watch closely.'

Some of the spilled coins glittered in the candlelight. The officer nodded. Assessing McHugh's condition, he gave his attention to affixing a length of cord about Lamont's wrists, first twisting them behind his back. Dan observed that he jerked the cord tight and made sure of the knot.

'Jail is three blocks down the street,' he commented. 'You'll appear in the morning to prefer charges?'

'I'll be there,' Dan promised.

'Fine.' He marched them from the room

39

and down the stairs, and the clerk, after an uncertain glance toward the money belt and spilled coins, made as if to follow, then hesitated.

'Do—you need anything?' he asked.

'Only to be left alone,' Dan returned. 'I'm apt to be nervous if awakened suddenly,' he added meaningly, and shut the door, placing a chair back under the knob. Having restored the coins to his money belt and the belt to its proper place, he sank down wearily on the bed. His head still throbbed, and presently he took the envelope from its hiding place and held the photograph to the light, studying it soberly.

'With all my love. Texas.'

Sighing, he blew out the candle.

The clerk, he was sure, would remain mute about the money belt, being far too timid to risk a try for it himself. He was less certain that Lamont and McHugh were the only enemies that he had in St. Louis.

By morning he felt reasonably like himself. As he had expected, McHugh and Lamont remained discreetly silent, admitting nothing, but offering no denial to the charges. McHugh's arm had been attended by a doctor and was in a sling. He looked wan and unhappy, but after a few days' rest would probably be as dangerous as ever.

Dan told his story of the attack and attempted robbery, which the officer backed.

The judge, plainly eager to be about some other task, took a thoughtful chew of tobacco, spat, and pronounced sentence.

'By rights, you more'n likely should be hung, the pair of you,' he observed. 'But probably, if ye keep on the way you've been, somebody else'll tend to that 'fore too long. Since you didn't get away with this, and one of you got lead poisonin', and since we can't have our jails too durned overcrowded, I sentence each of you to thirty days. That's all.'

It was as much as Dan had expected, and he was satisfied. It would keep them off his tail while he journeyed to Texas.

CHAPTER FIVE

By his own admission, E. Planchette was a gentleman adventurer, equally ready and able to live by his guns or his wits. There were those who disputed the first part of his self-bestowed accolade, but for them he had an airy contempt. E. Planchette's opinion of E. Planchette was so good that it was difficult to shake.

Even on this somewhat raw and foggy morning, when he awoke within the confines of the general jail in a not too respectable section of St. Louis, his self-confidence remained unshaken, despite the fact that, slowly adjusting himself to reality, he found the latter little to his liking.

For one thing, his head seemed overly large for his shoulders, while his temples throbbed with what might have been a severe hangover. That seemed unlikely, as he recalled having had only a single drink the evening before. To his practised palate, a single potion of fire-water was no more than a pleasant foretaste.

One drink, and only one, he thought ruefully. Rummaging through his pockets, he was dismayed but not surprised to find them empty.

It appears that I allowed myself to be duped and doped like the veriest tenderfoot, he decided with some amazement, and refrained from a chiding head shake at the enormity of the deception, for such movement was painful. That I should be so gullible! So now, as the price of carelessness, I find myself without funds, and in as squalid a place as this.

The situation required redress, and experience had taught him that it had to come through his own efforts. He looked about the room, surveying the other inmates.

Three of the six present he dismissed with weary distaste. They appeared to be like himself—bums who had been picked up for some disturbance and thrown into the lock-up to sleep it off. None was likely to possess any great potential for his profit. A fourth man, wearing a large checked vest and with a flashy ring upon his finger, he considered more carefully as being a borderline case. But the stone in the ring lacked the proper sparkle, and he dismissed him as unworthy.

The final two appeared more promising. They had retreated to a far corner of the room and were conferring together in low tones. Planchette, without appearing to do so, managed to hear. He prided himself on his ability to make excellent use of all his faculties.

'This is a mess,' Lamont growled. 'The best we can hope for is thirty days—and during that time, Rather will reach Texas and probably turn that paper over to Minifee. If he does, we're ruined.'

'I warned you to make sure of him,' McHugh retorted testily. 'First things first, always. But when you saw that money belt, you went crazy.'

Planchette pricked up his ears. A money belt was always doubly interesting. Lamont's reply was savage, despite his low tone.

'Is that so? It runs in my mind that you were just as interested in his gold as I was. And the way he went down when I hit him, he seemed to be out cold—any other man would have been Boothill bait. But digging graves for those not dead will do us no good.

It's stopping him now that's important.'

'Sure, but how do we manage it?' McHugh wondered. 'As you say, thirty days is the least we can hope for. He'll show up to testify against us, to keep us off his tail. You can be sure of that.'

'If we only had some money,' Lamont said wistfully. 'You can do a lot with money, by distributing it judiciously.'

'You've got something better than money,' McHugh reminded him: 'that ring we took off Vanstyne.'

'Don't be a fool. I made sure that they didn't find it when they searched me. If I flashed that, we'd really be in trouble, and to no purpose. It will be harder to change than a thousand-dollar bill.'

Planchette's thin nostrils quivered. He listened carefully as they continued to discuss the matter, noting with satisfaction that even so agile a pair of minds were unable to come up with a satisfactory solution to their problem. But then, feeling reasonably conversant with the situation and its possibilities, and since his own head had assumed manageable proportions, Planchette was ready to take a chance. At worst, he had nothing to lose. And the possibilities were intriguing.

He arose from his corner of the room, steadied himself, then leaned carefully to brush a bit of dried mud from his pants' knee. He sauntered across to where the other two sat, as far apart from the other inmates as they could manage. Not at all abashed by the scowls with which they greeted his approach, E. Planchette nodded affably.

'Good morning, gentlemen,' he greeted them. 'Generally speaking, of course. Permit me to introduce myself. I am E. Planchette—late of Louisville, Council Bluffs, New Orleans, Dog Town—or what have you. Name it and I've been there, or I'll find my way to it, for a proper reason and inducement. Planchette, gentleman adventurer, at your service.'

They regarded him with a growing interest, even a faint hopefulness, as he had intended. Without waiting for an invitation, he sat down on the floor beside them.

'First let me explain, gentlemen, that my hearing is acute—even excellent. I have listened with increasing interest to your conversation for the past quarter of an hour. Thus I perceive that you stand in need of a messenger, one ready and willing to act in your place—and foot-loose, as I expect to be, after the routine of a hearing within the next hour or so. I was brought in for being drunk. That was not exactly the case, but the charge is hardly of so serious a nature as to require my further detention.

'What must have happened—and the confession I find painful—is that someone fed

45

me knock-out drops, then robbed me. Thus I find myself in need of gainful employment, even as you require someone to do certain errands. And if you reason that so inept a bungler as I sound could be of no possible use to you, I can only plead that I was taken unawares. A first drink is usually the occasion for striking up an acquaintance. Ordinarily, I assure you, I am not gullible.'

McHugh and Lamont exchanged glances. Planchette read their thoughts and went on blandly.

'You do not quite credit what I have told you? Allow me to elaborate. A certain man—Rather—is heading for Texas. You want him stopped. I gather that he carries a well-filled money belt. That possibility is of course intriguing. But making sure of him would be easier if I had expense money, so as to travel by transportation equal to his. Unfortunately, as I have said, I was robbed last night. But now that we understand each other—why, if I may serve you gentlemen—' He smiled blandly.

They eyed each other and came to a decision. They had nothing to lose and much to gain.

'What you are suggesting, Mr. Planchette, might prove a risky—even a highly risky adventure,' Lamont suggested.

'So I gathered. But I am accustomed to such ventures.'

'It is of a confidential nature. We would require a most solemn promise that it would be carried out faithfully to the very end.'

Planchette smiled. 'If you want my oath on a Bible, gentlemen, I fear you will have to supply the Book. But you have my word as a gentleman that I will faithfully execute your wishes.'

'Ah yes, you are a *gentleman* adventurer?'

'I am, and I do not use the term lightly, sir. A man should give value received. The laborer is worthy of his hire—but he should prove trustworthy.'

'Then we'll take you up on your offer,' Lamont said. They filled him in more completely on the existing situation.

'What we require, sir, is that you stop Dan Rather from reaching Texas. How you do it—or what you do with such worldly goods as he may be carrying, which are considerable—is no concern of ours. We do want possession of a certain document which he carries. In addition, we would appreciate it if you would carry word of certain matters to a friend of ours who is associated in this venture with us—a man who lives as neighbor to the Minifees, in Texas: a Mr. Tilbury Jenkins.'

'What you ask seems reasonable,' Planchette agreed. 'Of course, it adds up to a great deal of time, work and responsibility. For that, I have a right to expect to be

47

adequately compensated. For the laborer *is* worthy of his hire.'

'Your reward will come with the accomplishment. Dan Rather's money belt is well filled.'

Planchette smiled and shook his head.

'That money belt is, shall we say, in the nature of my endeavor. I could go after it without regard to other bonus—after I have accomplished the dangerous part of matters. No, no, gentlemen, you misapprehend me. I must receive a substantial fee in advance.'

McHugh scowled. 'As we've pointed out, we have scarcely any money on us.'

'So I understand. But you do have something else—shall we refer to it as a pearl of great price?'

They eyed each other uncertainly, scowled and protested vociferously. But in the end, having no choice, they turned over the ring, which Planchette regarded with due admiration.

'Truly magnificent,' he breathed. 'Trust me, gentlemen. I will take every precaution in regard to the non-arrival of Major Rather in Texas.'

'See that you do,' McHugh growled. 'And don't forget that we'll follow you in due course.'

Planchette was elated. What had seemed like ill fortune might turn out to be very good luck indeed. Such a mission as he was undertaking was to his liking. First to be given a hearing, he was turned loose with the admonition to get out of town, which he cheerfully promised to do. Then he reminded his warder of certain personal property, and received his twin guns back in good shape.

He lingered a while in the courtroom, mingling with a group of spectators, while his employers were given thirty-day sentences, as they had expected. He was able to identify the chief witness against them as the man with whom he was to deal.

Taking care that Dan Rather should not see him, he returned to the street, and, regretfully pawning one of the pearl-handled revolvers, used the proceeds for certain necessary purchases, including passage on the stage west and, almost as an afterthought, a box of snuff.

He was a passenger on the stage when it pulled out later in the forenoon. Dan Rather rode opposite him.

Pleased with the detention of the pair for a thirty-day stay in St. Louis, Dan surveyed his fellow passengers carefully, but found no cause for suspicion.

Planchette chose to immerse himself in an old newspaper for the first hours of the ride. Oblivious to the swaying of the stage, he perused the news as zealously as though he had not read the same paper in detail only the day before. He shook his head over the

49

increasing uproar against the President. Finally, with a sigh, he folded the paper carefully, glanced around at his fellow passengers as though beholding them for the first time, and paused in the act of tucking the paper into an inner pocket.

'Er—pardon me. Would any of you care to look over this paper?' Though the query was addressed generally, he looked straight at Rather.

Dan smiled and shook his head. A somewhat blowsy woman, who might have been a farm wife or a scrub-woman, accepted the paper. She surprised everyone, when the coach halted shortly thereafter for the midday meal, by alighting and assuming charge as landlady, in the eating house. That incident served as a further excuse for breaking the ice, and Planchette took advantage of it, once they were back aboard the stage.

'I'd have pictured her in almost any other role,' he confessed, then made a wry face, 'at least until that greasy mutton and those mushy potatoes were served.'

'I noticed that she gave you an extra helping.' Dan grinned. They whiled away the afternoon in conversation, and by the time the stage halted for the night, Planchette knew that he had paved the way for eventual robbery.

It was the next forenoon, still well within the supposed boundaries of civilization and the law, that the unexpected happened. A shot rang out, fired warningly, and the stage pulled to a sudden halt. Two men, bearded and masked, confronted them as the passengers alighted and were lined up. One held a revolver; the other regarded them unwaveringly along the double barrels of a shotgun.

Planchette swore under his breath. It would seriously interfere with his plans should Dan Rather be robbed now.

Seven passengers were in the line. The driver remained on the box, both hands holding the reins, in full view. It appeared to Dan that he did not appear surprised or particularly discomfited; he seemed to be taking the robbery more supinely than necessary.

The man with the revolver started down the line, holding a sack in his other hand. Planchette was third in line, Dan Rather next.

The outlaw stopped in front of Planchette. His eyes gleamed at sight of the pearl-handled revolver, stuck in a sash about Planchette's waist.

'I'll take that toy,' he said. 'Toss it in my bag—and handle it like an egg, or my gun might go off. Now shell out whatever you've got.'

Planchette obeyed meekly. 'I'm a poor man, sir,' he protested. 'I possess but one small treasure. Surely you would not deprive a man of an heirloom, of small value save for the sake of sentiment?'

'Depends on what it is. Let's have a look.'

Planchette sighed again and fumbled in a coat pocket, well aware of the cocked revolver, whose cold eye stared between his own. But he had not been unduly boastful when assuring McHugh and Lamont that he possessed the qualities of an adventurer. He brought an object out carefully and unclasped his hand, and saw the outlaw's narrowed gaze start to widen, heard his snort of laughter, caused by mingled amusement and disgust. With a quick flick of the wrist, Planchette flung the contents of the snuff box full into his face.

The gun discharged as he had anticipated, but it was more from reflex action than by intention. The robber was blinded and choking. Planchette threw himself flat, hearing the whistle of the bullet overhead. He closed his arms about the bandit's legs and wrestled him to the ground.

He had not misjudged his traveling companion or his probable reaction. Dan Rather's derringer was in his hand, and the second outlaw was dropping his shotgun before its threat. A shot from one of the twin barrels of the little gun was a powerful persuader.

There was confusion, along with praise for

Planchette's heroism, followed by an acrimonious discussion as to what should be done with the prisoners. A drummer who had cowered silently until the danger was over, insisted that they should be hung from the nearest tree. The decision was made by Dan Rather to take them along to the nearest town and turn them over to the authorities.

'I'm indebted to you, suh,' Dan assured Planchette. 'I was not in a mood to be robbed, but the situation was difficult.'

'Think nothing of it, sir,' Planchette told him. 'My only regret is the waste of the snuff. In these unregenerate times, it is hard to come by—mighty hard to come by.'

CHAPTER SIX

It was typical of Randolph Minifee to disregard danger as though it did not exist. He had walked too long in the shadow of personal peril to heed it. It had pleased him when the news had reached him that his old friend and fellow officer, John Marston, had won a pardon for him from President Lincoln. The news was a weight off Texas' mind, and that made it worth-while.

The news had reached them some time ago, through sources too authentic to doubt. But the actual pardon was being carried by

53

Colonel Marston, and until such times as he arrived and removed the risk of arrest, Minifee chose simply to disregard the threat.

Today, long black coattails flapping, full patriarchal black beard flowing across his chest, Minifee was essaying a feat which most of his ranch hands preferred not to try. Crimson Satan, a three-year-old whose father was an Arabian, his mother a range cayuse, had been brought in from the range for breaking. Among the hands he was called the Red Devil, and with reason.

This was the third time in a year that an attempt was being made to tame him. On the first occasion he had thrown Old Charley, the best broncobuster in Texas; then, ears laid back wickedly and hoofs bunched, had stomped him, before anyone could come to Charley's rescue.

The second try had been even more devastating, ending in a break for freedom which had left Satan the leader of a wild bunch, to run free for half a year. Now he was bridled again, and saddled under the supervision of Lamarie, who served as foreman under Minifee. The general himself was riding the Red Devil. To the surprise of no one, he was doing it with the same reckless ease with which he managed almost everything. The first half-dozen jumps of the big red appeared to be almost half-hearted.

Then, so suddenly as to take even Minifee

by surprise, the pony became a plunging, whirling, screaming devil, living up to his name. The times when Minifee had been unseated were few, but this was one of them. He hit the ground hard, started to rise, then fell back, groaning. A dozen of the crew, watchfully alert, kept the killer horse away.

Texas was the first to reach her father's side. Looking anxious yet demure, and twice as pretty as her picture, she had been perched, along with some of the men, on the topmost rail of the corral. She was off it with a ballooning of skirts, across the intervening space and kneeling, all in a moment.

Minifee's tan seemed to have paled, but he managed a reassuring smile at sight of her tense face.

'Don't get the wind up, girl. Broke a leg, I guess. Might as easy have been my fool neck.'

Assured that it was no worse, Texas assumed charge. 'Get a door off the barn for a stretcher,' she commanded. 'Then get him to the house.' She watched while that was done, then turned to look at the red pony, now standing, shivering with reaction, not far away. For a moment the men, knowing her tempestuous nature, expected to hear an order to shoot the outlaw.

Instead, Texas moved toward the horse, her eyes narrowing. A couple of the crew moved swiftly to hold it fast by the bridle reins. Lamarie Jones, his square face as bleak as rough-hewed granite, ventured a word of caution.

'He's a tricky devil, Miss Texas, not to be trusted.'

Her answer was to seize a stirrup, hooking it up over the saddle-horn. Then, with a quick jerk, she loosened the cinch and reached under the edge of the saddle blanket. Now the others saw what she had been first to notice. The blanket was discolored by a fresh stain at that point, of the same color as Red Devil's hair.

The horse stood quietly as she pulled loose a heavy, dry burr. It was partly crushed, wet with blood where it had been forced into the flesh, but the spines were still sharp and ugly. Holding it, she swung back, and her eyes were sharp with anger.

'Who placed this under the saddle?' she demanded. 'No wonder he went crazy.' Her gaze rested accusingly on Lamarie. 'I'm surprised that you didn't notice something wrong, Lamarie.'

Lamarie's leathery face went red with embarrassment, and he had no word of excuse. There was some justification for having failed to notice it, of course. The burr had been so placed that it would be only mildly uncomfortable until the full weight of a rider came into the saddle. So well had it been set that Crimson Satan had taken his first couple of bucks without much annoyance. There had been just the normal pitching of a horse which had long gone unridden.

Only when his pitching had brought the full weight of the rider jolting down had the burr cut savagely, sending him into the wild pitching motion which had followed.

The half-hearted manner in which he had bucked at the start took on new significance. It suggested that someone must have tormented the pony in similar fashion on other occasions, without the trick being detected.

'Father had planned to ride him both those other times,' Texas blazed at the men. 'Only Charley figured to gentle him a bit first—and the Kid had to show off! This time it worked—the plan to cripple the general just when he's being hunted!'

Her eyes swept the assembled crew, then fixed on the tall Javits. The others looked, too, and under that battery of glances, Javits grew red, then paled. His eyes shifted and his feet shuffled.

'I supposed we had a loyal crew here on Randolph Ranch,' Texas said accusingly. 'Why did you do it?'

Javits' mouth opened as though in denial. But everyone remembered that he had saddled the red horse each time, and in the light of the new revelation they were also remembering other things.

'I like to see good bucking,' he said sullenly.

It was a clumsy lie. Javits turned and began to run, paying no heed when Lamarie ordered him to halt. He was almost at the corner of the barn when a revolver blasted, and Javits sprawled in a twisting fall. Lamarie blew smoke from his gun.

'Just drilled his leg,' he explained. 'Maybe I should have aimed higher.'

'You did fine,' Texas commended him. 'I want him to answer some questions.'

'He'll sure get a chance to unburden himself,' Lamarie agreed heavily. 'Must be some of them Yankee carpetbaggers hired him to do a trick like that.'

The next hour was a busy one, while Texas and Lamarie together set the broken leg of the general, then splinted it carefully. She worked expertly, showing no emotion or sign of fainting until it was done. But her eyes were thoughtful, and they did not warm as a new arrival came stamping into the house.

Tilbury Jenkins strode forward, a big, overconfident man whose heartiness overflowed. It was his custom to make himself at home on Randolph Ranch, doing so with the assurance of a cousin once removed. Unlike most men, he heeded the lightning which flashed from the eyes of Texas no more than Sheridan had been impressed by the far-off rumble of cannon on

58

a certain fateful ride.

Before she could draw back, he captured Texas' hands, then held them tight in his own big paws, gazing down at her solicitously.

'You poor gal,' he exclaimed. 'I just heard the news about your Pa's bustin' his leg, Texas. And I reckon I don't need to tell you how down right upsettin' that is.'

'I can guess,' Texas returned dryly. She freed her hands and drew back. Then, conscious of her obligations as a hostess, she seated herself. Tilbury Jenkins took another chair, crossing long legs in front of him. He gazed admiringly at the shiny leather of his boots.

'Brand-new boots,' he confided. 'I got old Andy to make me a pair. Sure needed them, for I was the next thing to going barefooted!' His smile faded. 'I rode over because I've got news for you, Texas. Not too good, either—for which I'm almighty sorry. But I figured you'd want to know, so I didn't waste no time.'

Despite herself, Texas' face lost color. News, for the past half year, had been almost uniformly bad. The rare good reports had been more than matched by the gloomy ones.

A general amnesty for those who had fought for the South had appeared to be in effect after Lee had surrendered, and it had seemed that this included her father. Hopes had been bright that, with the war finally over and the senseless slaughter stopped, they might begin the long process of rebuilding.

Such hopes had proved premature. With Lincoln slain, and Johnson all but helpless in the hands of his enemies, reprisals were the order of the day. Now her father lay crippled, and this obnoxious cousin spoke of more bad news.

'What is it?' she asked.

'I don't rightly know where to begin,' Jenkins confessed, and gave a twist to his mustache. 'I reckon you know that I've been mighty concerned about the gen'ral, Texas. I used all my influence to persuade Colonel Marston to work to get a pardon for him. But I don't need to tell you that.'

Texas offered neither denial nor agreement. He did not need to tell her, having already assured her of his activity at least a score of times. It had been unsought aid, which she was certain had had no effect whatever on John Marston. Since he was the sort of man he was, she could guess that such gratuitous advice had probably disgusted and angered him. But, being John Marston, he would have gone ahead regardless.

'Well, you know how he wangled a pardon from Old Abe, just before that Yankee got what was comin' to him,' Jenkins continued. 'The way things were then, Marston figured it'd be a heap better just to bring that pardon out here himself, not entrustin' it to no mail

60

nor nobody. Anyhow, we decided that was the way to do it, and I figured to take as many precautions as I could, to see that the colonel got here all right with it. Near as I can figure, though, he didn't do all the things I said. The colonel was mighty stiff-necked, and he liked to do things his own way, no matter how foolish it was.'

Texas' breath caught. She leaned forward.

'What do you mean, *was*?' she demanded. 'Has something happened to Colonel Marston?'

Tilbury Jenkins nodded gloomily. 'That's one of the things I had to tell you,' he admitted. 'I'm afraid it has. When he wouldn't rightly heed good advice, to protect his own neck, I did the best I could. I arranged for a friend of mine to travel right along with him—without lettin' him know or suspect, of course. This friend was to keep an eye out for trouble, and help the colonel if he could in case trouble did come. It was sure lucky that I did—though he wasn't able to help much, as it turned out.'

'What happened?' Texas' voice was quiet, too calm, but Jenkins failed to notice.

'Well, the colonel got on a river boat, bound for St. Louis. And somebody shot him in his cabin one night.'

Texas' breath expelled in an anguished gasp. 'You mean he was killed?'

Jenkins nodded heavily. 'Murdered,' he

growled. 'As near as could be learned, he was shot by a man named Rather—Dan Rather—'

'Dan Rather? Oh, it couldn't be!'

Jenkins regarded her suspiciously. 'Why not? What's his name got to do with a man being a murderin' scoundrel?'

'I doubt if there could be two Dan Rathers,' Texas explained. 'It's an unusual name. And Old Dan Rather—haven't you heard of him? He was a famous fighter on our side. When I was back there to visit Father during the struggle, I heard a lot about him—a song they sang, all sorts of things.'

'Sounds like him, all right,' Jenkins conceded. 'Major Dan Rather. According to the word I got, he and the colonel hated each other. And I reckon he'd got word about what Marston carried. Seems like he got hold of it, too—the pardon that the colonel was bringing out here.'

The long, slender nails of either hand bit into the flesh of each pink palm. Otherwise Texas gave no sign. 'Go on,' she ordered.

'That's most of it,' Jenkins conceded. 'My friend didn't manage to save the colonel, he being so set on doing things his way, or to keep him from being robbed. But he did make sure that this Dan Rather was headin' this way—and sent me word.'

'It doesn't make sense,' Texas protested. 'If he murdered a man as prominent as Colonel Marston, on board a river boat, and was known—surely he would be arrested and tried for the crime.'

'Seems that way, but I guess nobody actually saw it done, and there was no evidence to hold him on. But the fact that he's heading out here now speaks for itself. With that pardon in his possession, he likely figures to blackmail you for plenty—special with all these worthless Yankee carpetbaggers closin' in like they are. So it's mighty lucky we know what to expect.'

'You're sure about all this?'

'I wish I wasn't.' Tilbury sighed. 'I sure hate to bring bad news. But when we're warned what to expect, we can prepare and act according. And there's disturbin' news closer home, when it comes to that.'

'More?'

'Well, it ain't *too* bad—but there's a Captain Culdeen in town, a Yankee. 'Course, he ain't sayin' what he's after, but I guess it's plain enough what he's in this neck of the woods for.'

Texas nodded. It was much too plain—to arrest the general and pack him off to a rigged trial and death. That sort of thing was becoming increasingly common, particularly in the case of men who still retained sufficient wealth to make them worth such attention. Frequently their property was seized as belonging to traitors. It was highly irregular and often illegal, but the new holders of

63

power used it ruthlessly.

Jenkins stood up and came closer. He made another attempt to capture her hands, but Texas eluded him.

'I sure hate to be the bringer of bad news, Texas, sweetheart,' he asserted. 'But I figured you ought to know soon as possible. And with all this trouble and your Pa down flat, it's up to me more'n anybody else to look out for you. That being so—well, you know how much I've always cared for you, honey. So maybe we better give me the right to act. Right now, more'n ever, you need me to look after you. Just say the word, Texas, and I'll stand between you and the whole Yankee army!'

Texas glanced at him askance. Remembering the whispered stories concerning guerilla activity in which he was said to have indulged during the war, bringing down upon himself the hatred of both sides, Texas doubted what a stand would amount to. But he had been clever enough to cover his trail, so that evidence was lacking.

Her impulse was to slap him for his presumption, to express her feelings as forcibly as she could. But with troubles increasing and dangers piling up on every side, she could not afford needlessly to antagonize him. She drew back, smiling even as she shook her head.

'What sort of talk is that, Tilbury? And you and I are cousins!'

'Second cousins,' Jenkins reminded her. 'And I'm mighty proud of it! But that makes no matter. We need each other, Texas, and you need me to take care of you and the place here. I couldn't ask for nothin' more—'

'You know that I'm too busy even to think of such matters now,' Texas reproved him. 'And besides—after just receiving the news about poor Colonel Marston—'

Jenkins scowled, then twisted his mouth into a smile.

'Yeah, sure I know,' he conceded. 'I suppose this does hit you kind of hard, coming so sudden. And I guess I shouldn't hold nothin' against him, 'special now that he's dead. But it strikes me that he was doing what he was not so much through friendship for your Pa as to get *you*, and him twice your age! Anyhow, all you ever felt for him was gratitude and maybe a sense of obligation, but that's out of the way now. What's happened has happened, so there ain't a thing in the world to keep you from marryin' me, and I sure intend that you shall!'

Up till then, Texas had given him no more than half her attention. Now she turned, her eyes intent.

'Don't count on it,' she warned, then softened the refusal a trifle. 'There's no profit in storing up disappointments for yourself.'

CHAPTER SEVEN

Snuff was difficult to come by almost anywhere along the frontier. Therefore the scattering to the wind of a full box of dust seemed an abominable waste. But in spite of his loss, Planchette was well satisfied. The sacrifice had served a double purpose. Not only had he foiled the hold-up, with its incipient threat of disaster, but by the act he had gained the confidence both of the driver of the stage and, more importantly, of Dan Rather.

They went on, and Planchette put his new status to good use. He was first out of the door whenever the stage halted, lending a helping hand hooking or unhooking a team, assisting greasing the wheels, making himself generally useful. As they neared the end of the run, it became a simple matter to insert a slab of sharp stone between the fetlock and the shoe of the off wheeler. Adjusted in such fashion, the stone might work loose before it caused any damage. But the probability was that it would work its way through the hair and into the flesh.

It worked as he had planned, causing the horse to go lame within a few miles. Even after the stone was found and removed, the lameness remained, slowing the whole team to a limping pace. At this juncture, Planchette made another helpful suggestion.

'Country like this, with change stations so far apart, we'll lose hours 'fore we get a replacement,' he observed sympathetically. 'Tell you what. Let me take one of the team and ride on to the next station. I'll send back a fresh team; in the long run, it'll save time.'

Since by now the lamed animal could barely travel, the suggestion made sense. While the others waited, Planchette rode ahead. True to his promise, he delivered the message and promptly despatched the attendant back with fresh horses.

Having fulfilled his obligation, he was alone, in charge of the change house, until the stage should overtake him. Anything which he might do in the interval would go unobserved.

He had neglected to explain his familiarity with the distances between stations, or to mention that he had previously visited that section of the country. His acquaintance was considerably more than superficial.

Red men as well as white had been restless during the years of strife, with allegiances frequently uncertain. Since then, as Planchette was well aware, the coming of peace had scarcely stabilized the situation. Ostensibly the red men were children of the Great White Father, and under his care; but that benign guardian was at best a shadowy figure, and the hands through which he worked were frequently bungling.

Still, the government did try. It had established an agency not many miles distant from the stage station, with an agent who was supposed to placate the Indians, to look after their interests as well as those of the white men, and thus preserve the cause of peace.

On a fairly recent visit to the section, Planchette had made the agent's acquaintance, finding in him a kindred soul, and prolonging his stay from a matter of hours to days. It would be no more than courtesy to look in now on an old friend—especially since Planchette had discovered the agent to be a carpetbagger at heart.

Helping himself to a fresh horse from the stock kept at the station, Planchette rode to find the agent. He hoped to complete his errand and be back before the stage arrived, but that was a secondary consideration. An errand for Jacques Cousins came first.

His luck was really running high. Being robbed and arrested in St. Louis had seemed a strange way of receiving the Lady's favors, but now he realized that it was the best thing which had happened to him in a long while. Not only did he find the agent at home and in his office, but as an added bonus, Mr. Cousins was relatively sober. Jacques stared in disbelief, then, convinced that it was no

68

illusion, greeted him warmly.

'I never expected to see you back in this country again,' he explained. 'I figured that by now they'd probably have hung you.'

The subject was touchy, even when branched with levity, but Planchette brushed it aside with a smile.

'Not a chance,' he asserted. 'My luck is too good for that. And the reason that I'm here is because there's a chance for you and me to split a nice sum of money between us. Exactly how much I'm not sure, but from reports, I estimate that there's several thousand dollars—in gold. Why should it travel through the country, instead of remaining with those who would properly appreciate it?'

Cousins' heavy face showed animation. He wet his lips with an eager tongue.

'Gold?' he repeated. 'Any talk of money always makes sense. Who's got it?'

'It's in the money belt of one of the passengers on the stage—which has been delayed.' Planchette explained the reasons, including his insertion of the bit of rock to lame the horse. 'So the stage will be along in due course. What remains is the transfer of the belt from Dan Rather to ourselves.'

Planchette had considered it an innocuous name. Its effect upon Cousins was startling. He drew back as though remembering the injunction to look not upon the wine when it was red.

'Rather? Did you say Dan Rather?' he repeated.

'That's his name,' Planchette agreed. 'A former major in the forces of Jeff Davis. Why?'

'I've heard of him,' the agent protested. 'And if it's the same man—and it sounds like it might be—I ain't interested. I wouldn't want to tangle with Old Dan Rather for a dozen money belts bulgin' with gold.'

Planchette regarded him with pained disbelief.

'And I was counting on you!' he protested. 'All the crying in your beer about lack of opportunities—your wasted years in the wilderness—and now, when I come with opportunity on both hands, you shrink like a chunk of rawhide in the sun! You don't suppose that I have neglected to formulate a plan, do you—a fool-proof one with a minimum of risk?'

Cousins' tongue moved uncertainly, but with a trace of eagerness. 'Well,' he wavered, 'if you've got a plan—'

'I have, and with the details all worked out. I managed to do Dan Rather a favor the other day, and I think I'm not unduly boastful when I say that he holds me in some esteem. We will be on the stage together when it goes on. All that you have to do is send some of your restless braves to attack the stage and massacre everyone on board—except me. For them, it will be the sort of pleasant diversion which they have found all too rare of late.'

The agent's florid color showed signs of fading. He wet his lips again in a flurry of nervousness.

'Diversion?' he stammered. 'Massacre—of the stage! Why, that would be going pretty far. Besides, it's terribly risky!'

Planchette shrugged.

'Risky? When you're sitting here, safe at home, while others do all the work? I gathered during my recent sojourn here that some of your charges looked upon you with no great degree of enthusiasm. This way, you can earn their gratitude and even a measure of respect.'

'But there's more than the Indians. It would be sure to excite indignation—bring repercussions—'

'Yes. I suppose that's inevitable,' Planchette acknowledged. 'But I don't see where there's a risk. *You'll* be the one to make all necessary inquiries into the affair—and the noble red men will be the only witnesses.'

Tempted, Cousins considered. His tongue moved more recklessly.

'Well—that's so. But there's another risk. That sort of thing could stir the warriors into wanting more of the same. A taste of blood, you know. For they're still savages at heart—'

'Well, I can probably manage some other

way.' Planchette shrugged. 'E. Planchette has had a lot of experience. Since we were passing through this part of the country, I remembered you, as a friend, and I thought you'd like to share in an easy windfall. But I can use the whole amount of gold for myself instead of dividing it.'

He let himself out through the door and started to untie his horse. Cousins hesitated, then followed to pluck at his sleeve.

'Wait,' he protested urgently. 'I didn't say it couldn't be worked. I appreciate your thinking of me—and of course I like to help a friend in such a case. But just how do you figure the final part of it can be managed?'

He listened, shivering anew as Planchette explained in detail, but he had already committed himself.

'All right, I'll tend to it,' he promised. 'There's time enough, and it sounds all right. Only it's such a devilish scheme! And you never did tell me what the E in your name stands for.'

Planchette smiled, pulling himself back into the saddle. Not in long years had he acknowledged the Ebenezer. Cousins quailed as he leaned down.

'What does it stand for?' he mocked. 'Why, for Evil, of course. What else?'

CHAPTER EIGHT

Fury was in the swirl of her skirts as Texas strode back toward the house—a mannish, purposeful stride, in contrast with her usual sedate pace. Lamarie, rounding a corner of the barn, stopped at sight of her, his own face more sharp and craggy than the three-day growth of whiskers justified.

'Miss Texas—what's wrong?'

'Javits has escaped,' she stormed. 'I ordered him locked up—and he couldn't have broken out unless someone helped him! I intended to have the truth out of him as to who paid him to place that burr under the saddle!'

Lamarie nodded gravely. He was foreman, but in this crisis, with her father's life and honor at stake, Texas was taking over authority as naturally as the wind swept across the plains. He accepted it without resentment, even with a sense of pride.

'I'll set about findin' him,' he promised.

'Do that. He'll tell the truth—or hang!' Texas blazed. 'I'm fed up, Lamarie. It's bad enough to have the Yankees hounding Dad, as they are doing—but to have traitors, double-crossers in our own midst! I'm going to discover who's back of all this—and when I do, he'll wish *he* was in the hands of the

Yankees instead!'

Lamarie did not doubt it. Treachery to one's own land, to one's outfit, came close to being the unforgivable sin. The South was prostrate, but that was nothing new; poverty could be endured with no lessening of pride. It was when sons of the South turned to plot with the oppressor, whatever their motive, that conditions grew insupportable.

'I'll find him,' he promised again grimly. 'I'm honin' to hear what he has to say, myself.'

There was no sound, at least none audible to their ears at that distance, but a puff of dust showed, becoming a moving streak, more than a quarter of a mile away, near the foot of the long slope beyond the buildings. It was topped in turn by maze of brush which was at once a landmark of the country and a trial to the cattlemen. Texas' raking glance caught the dust, and her breath jerked.

'There he is!' she cried. 'He's getting away!'

Even Lamarie's gaze, trained to withstand sun and storm and the wideness of an endless land, hesitated momentarily upon the distant rider. Then he saw that Texas was right; it was Javits who was putting distance between himself and the buildings as rapidly as a horse could gallop.

'I'll get him,' Lamarie repeated for a third time, and started to run for the open doors of

74

the barn, where a horse most quickly could be found.

Texas did not even glance after him. Lamarie was a good man, and he'd follow a trail relentlessly, but he was set in his ways, and he'd be too slow. Once among the all but impenetrable brush, Javits would disappear as completely as a wild longhorn. With so much of a head start, something faster than another horse was needed.

An instrument was at hand. Old Jose ambled into sight, a rifle slung across his shoulder. Jose was the best mountain lion killer in all of Texas, the most relentless foe of the lean tawny hunters. For his prowess in depleting the ranks of the cattle killers, Randolph Minifee had presented him with the latest model repeating rifle.

Texas' apology followed her snatch of the gun. 'I need this,' she said, and leveled it, sighting along the barrel. An instant later lightning leaped from its muzzle, and the warning bullet buzzed at the nose and ears of the running cayuse—lead so well aimed that the pony snorted and swerved. Before the thunder of the rifle had even reached his ears, Javits jerked it savagely back on course and goaded with digging spurs.

One warning was all that could be expected, especially since the shelter of the brush was only jumps away. Texas' second shot seemed to blend with the sound of the first, and the distant horse faltered in its stride, made a gallant effort to recover, then went down in a sprawling tumble. Javits, caught, was pinned fast. His injured limb precluded a quick jump from the saddle.

Lamarie checked his run short of the barn, staring from the horseman to Texas and back again. Texas blew smoke from the open barrel of the rifle, clicked it shut and handed it back to Jose.

'Thanks, Jose,' she said. 'I couldn't have managed with a less sweet-shooting rifle. You have rendered a great favor to Randolph Ranch, to the general and myself. I think he'll wait while you fetch him,' she added to Lamarie.

Jose was grinning broadly, his face shining like polished saddle leather. 'It is the good gun, *si*?' He nodded. 'But even I cannot better such a shot as that, Miss Texas.'

'Too bad it had to be his horse,' Texas returned, and now, for just an instant, her lip quivered. 'But it was him or the horse—and I want him alive, to talk!'

Lamarie was already mounted and riding. He returned presently, accompanied by half a dozen more members of the crew. Javits was seated sullenly on another horse, his hands tied behind his back. The bandage which had been applied to the fleshy part of his leg was stained, but he could bear his weight upon it.

'He wan't much hurt by the spill,' Lamarie

explained. 'Got pinned in some brush, and it took most of the weight of the horse. Given a little more time, he'd have wriggled loose same as a snake.'

'He's as slippery as a sidewinder,' Texas agreed, studying the scowling face of Javits. 'But this time, Javits, you aren't going to get away, at least not until you've answered my question, and I want the truth. Who paid you for this treachery?'

Javits had regained his aplomb. He was scratched and bruised, and his wounded leg throbbed, but his second escape within an hour had convinced him that his luck was good. There had been an instant, after the whining buzz of the first bullet, the shock of the second and the horse going down, when fear had plagued him. Now he was reassured. Had it been the general who was asking the questions, it might have been bad. But in a showdown, he could outbluff any woman. Texas was too tender-hearted to take drastic action.

'I like to see how good a horse can buck, how good a man can ride,' he said.

'Well, you saw,' Texas replied. 'And so did the rest of us. Now we'll see how long you can dance on air. Jose, throw a rope over the big limb of that tree.'

Old Jose obeyed, smiling cheerfully, his rope's end sailing true over a high limb at the first try. Next to his ability as a lion hunter,

77

Jose prided himself most on his skill with a rope. Following the shot just made with his rifle, his devotion to the Lady of Texas had increased almost to worship. If she wanted to hang a man, then it was a privilege to hold the rope.

Some of the ruddiness faded from under Javits' tan, but he maintained his air of indifference as the others, following Texas' gesture, aided him beneath the tree and adjusted the noose over his head. One assisted him to balance himself with a hand on an arm, a consideration scarcely appreciated. But Javits had played a lot of poker, and he understood the value of bluff.

'Talk—or swing!' Texas snapped. Her face was white, but her voice was sharp with controlled anger. Javits smiled mockingly. The grin jerked off like a mask as she gestured, and the men at the other end of the rope pulled. They halted only when his feet dangled just above the ground.

He kicked wildly with his uninjured leg, gyrating madly, eyes protruding, face reddening as his wind was cut off. The torment was real and the terror worse, as he struggled desperately with the rope which held his wrists. Texas watched, her face inscrutable. Deep inside, she was sickened and revolted, but for the moment she was in charge of Randolph Ranch, and the stakes were high. They included her father's life and, she had come darkly to suspect, perhaps much more. And with the crew infested with traitors, who would place a burr as Javits had done, or release him from prison before he could be questioned—

Lamarie's knuckles showed white where his hands held a length of the rope, and sweat glistened on his face. He glanced questioningly at Texas, then at the man whose struggles were suddenly subsiding. Texas nodded, and they relaxed the rope with signs of relief.

Javits' feet were on the ground, but he swayed drunkenly and would have pitched forward except for the steadying effect of a hand upon his arm. His eyes goggled, and Texas nodded to the man who assisted him.

'Loose the rope so that he can breathe,' she commanded.

A thumb was inserted, and the others eyed her with awe and increased respect. Many of them had watched her play with dolls, or turn from them to ride a pony at a headlong pace. They had seen her bake a mouthwatering pie, or tie a calf as quickly and surely as any man in the crew. But this was a Texas they had never known.

Javits swayed, gasping, lungs heaving. Slowly he gained a semblance of normality, was able to think again, tensely aware that the noose was still about his neck, the rough strands prickling suggestively. The other end was still gripped by those who had dragged him to what had seemed a vast height between earth and sky. He wet his lips with a darting tongue, and searched in vain for any sign of mercy, of relenting, in the faces of the men or the woman. Those of the men were carefully blank, but admiration was in their eyes.

'All that you have to do is tell who hired you,' Texas informed him. 'Then you can ride—as far as you like. But if they drag you up again, you won't come down alive!'

Fear flashed in his eyes for the first time, and he made his decision.

'All right, I'll tell you,' he croaked. 'I didn't bargain for anything like this. You ought to be able to guess,' he went on mockingly, 'seein' who—'

This time his luck had run out. His open mouth gushed sudden red, and his head jerked like a melon to the impact of the bullet. When, an instant later, the roar of the rifle sounded from a distance, it was already over. Someone had freed Javits to make sure that he did not tell what he knew. The first time it had failed, but this time the insurance was complete. Javits would name no names, now or ever.

CHAPTER NINE

When the stagecoach belatedly reached the stop, with the lame horse trotting behind, E. Planchette was waiting. He emerged from the cabin, yawning and rubbing his eyes.

'Well, I see you made it all right,' he observed. 'And I've sure had a good sleep, waiting here. Best I've had in a long while.'

'You mean to say that all you've done is sleep?' the driver demanded enviously.

'That's it,' Planchette agreed placidly. 'With nobody around to bother me, I've made the most of my opportunities.'

Dan Rather looked at him curiously. Today he was taking a turn, assisting with the horses, helping stable the extra animals before they should go on. He had observed a horse already in the barn, a saddle pony, standing before a fresh stall full of hay. Only it was not eating. Its flanks still heaved from a long run, and a coat of sweat was only partially dry. When a horse was too exhausted even to nibble at hay, it had been driven hard.

Since the others had failed to notice, Dan made no observation. According to his own account, Planchette had spent all his time sleeping, with no one to disturb him. The hard-ridden cayuse indicated otherwise.

For his own part, it would pay to be both

wakeful and watchful. Planchette had been most friendly and helpful. But Yank and Reb soldiers could exchange pleasantries during a lull in the fighting, then shoot with no less deadly intent once the battle resumed.

Delayed as the stage had been, it would arrive late at the next change house, the first station with over-night accommodations for the passengers. They were due before sunset, but the moon would be high by the time they arrived.

As night came down, the other passengers composed themselves as comfortably as possible and tried to sleep. One or two apparently succeeded. Dan Rather made a pretense of dozing and observed that Planchette was doing the same. For a man who by his own account had spent most of the day sleeping, he seemed unnaturally drowsy.

The attack came as suddenly as had the prior one, with one notable difference. Instead of a command to halt, guns made a clamor, and under the treacherous fusillade the driver went over the side, bouncing against the wheel before striking the ground. No hand remained upon the reins, but the horses did not run. A horde of shadowy figures converged upon the team from either side, seizing bridle reins, halting the cayuses before they could panic. And now a new and more terrible clamor overrode the guns—the wild noise of a war whoop.

Hands tore eagerly at the doors, and gun barrels were thrust inside, blasting wildly as they came. Dan Rather emptied his guns in turn, picking his targets with cool precision. He'd learned long since that a single well-placed shot could be more effective than a hundred fired at random, and he cleared a way at one door, then got through it and into the darkness. There he promptly faded into the shadows, crouching down and reloading. He was careful not to try to go far.

The sound of the war whoops ended, and the fight was over as abruptly as it had started. For a while Indians continued to mill about, busy with tasks which it was no pleasure to watch. Since there were no further sounds of life about the stage, Dan held his fire.

Finally they were gone. He returned to the scene, viewing the carnage grimly. Identification was no longer easy, but one victim was unmistakably Planchette. Certain of that, Dan wondered if he had misjudged him.

Then, looking closer, he glimpsed something which caught and held even the faint glimmers of light. To view it fully it was necessary to turn Planchette on his side. As he fell, his right hand had been almost under him, thus escaping notice. But on one finger was a ring which had not been there earlier in the evening. Possibly it had been slipped on as a sign or means of identification.

Whatever the reason, Dan had seen it before, on board the *Mississippi Belle*. How it came to be on Planchette's finger was a riddle as intriguing as it was grim. But he knew that he was not mistaken. This was the ring which had been euchred from Vanstyne.

★   ★   ★

The shadow of horror lingered in the eyes of Texas when she entered the house some time later. Though prompt and thorough, the search for Javits' killer had been in vain. Actually, she had expected nothing else. Javits had been a tool, useful to a certain point but not particularly clever, and therefore ruthlessly discarded when he became a liability to his employer.

The ambush bullet had been fired from quite close at hand, but the killer had planned well. He had stood on a well-beaten path, then had kept on it, to lose himself among the clustering brush and trees of the rough country. He probably still lay hidden within sound of their voices, but an army might search such terrain in vain. The odds were good that he had deliberately mingled with the searchers.

With his last breath, Javits had given a clue, only it was not quite good enough. Texas knew that she should be able to guess, but the difficulty was that she could make a dozen guesses; and suspicion, even active dislike or hatred, was no sure method for determining guilt. Emotions could be unworthy substitutes for truth.

One fact, however, stood out more starkly than before, exactly as Tilbury Jenkins had warned. This was a struggle for control and the possession of Randolph Ranch. With such high stakes, her father, his life, even she herself were no more than pawns on the board. The ramifications of the contest had already reached to the national capital, had spread to encompass murder on a river boat, and had risen to a bloody crest here in Texas.

And the end, she realized with a coldness about her heart, was not yet.

She glanced from a window, then went quickly to the door. Lamarie Jones was approaching the house with strides so long that he was all but running.

'One of the boys just got back from town, and he heard something there,' Lamarie said breathlessly. 'There's a Yankee captain just come to town—Culdeen, they say his name is, Rab Culdeen. Leastwise, he *was* in town. Then he set out this way, with a dozen or so Yankee soldiers at his back. Bob, he cut around him to bring word; they ain't far off.'

Texas' hand flew to her throat. This, too, was as Tilbury had warned. Captain Culdeen might be only a soldier who strove to do his

85

duty according to orders, but that duty for the moment would include the discovery and arrest of Randolph Minifee. Once that was accomplished, her father's life would be as surely forfeit as Javits' had been. If his death was achieved, a giant stride would have been taken toward the stealing of his possessions.

'Most of our boys done some soldierin', and they ain't forgot how to fight,' Lamarie suggested. 'You want we should sort of get in the way of them Yankees?'

Texas shook her head. 'That would only make matters worse,' she pointed out, and saw in Lamarie's eyes that he felt the same. She had been about to go to the room where, at her orders, her father had been taken. With his injured limb attended to, she hoped he was resting comfortably.

Now such a visit, to undertake a discussion of plans and strategy, was too late. If the soldiers were on the way, there was no time to be lost. Either to argue or plead with her father would be a waste of breath. Randolph Minifee was a gentleman, and aristocrat of the old school. He had shown courage and initiative countless times, and in a game with the enemy he did not deign to go in disguise or to resort to legitimate strategy. That was all a part of war.

To skulk or run like a coward, even to preserve his own life, was not to be considered. He simply would not do such a thing. He'd sit up in bed with a brace of revolvers and face his adversaries, and it might depend on the circumstances of the moment whether he surrendered with a shrug or whether he died and, in a final burst of fighting, took as many with him as he could contrive.

Since it was too late for argument, there were other methods. To these Texas had prudently given forethought, making such preparations as seemed feasible. Now she reached a decision.

'Spread the word, Lamarie, that the general's injury wasn't as bad as we'd feared; just a sprain. He can still ride. But pass it softly, Lamarie—and discreetly.'

Lamarie studied her face, and some of the anxiety faded from his own. He had always loved the tomboyish heiress to the big ranch, and of late he had come increasingly to respect her judgment and ability. Since she had a plan, that was good enough for him.

'Whatever you say, Miss Texas. It won't be hard to drop a word along those lines.'

'Then get on with it, Lamarie. We've no time to lose.'

She turned abruptly and was gone. In her own room, she dragged a chest from beneath the bed, spread part of the contents out, and then worked swiftly, efficiently. She studied herself in a mirror as she changed to an outfit similar to that worn by her father only that morning.

Loitering near the barn, Lamarie watched and waited both for possible orders and for the appearance of the unwelcome Yankees. Unless instructions to the contrary were received, he knew what his course must be—to receive the Yankee captain politely, and to be prepared for whatever might come to pass. Texas had a plan, and if he'd had any doubts during the past weeks, this day's events had removed them. With the general incapacitated, Texas was the boss.

He caught the glint of sun on sidearms, the flash of blue uniforms as soldiers jogged into sight, following the road from town, appearing along an avenue between tall oaks, nearly a mile away. He estimated their number at a score, and he watched with his heart suddenly in his throat as he saw another horseman, this one a lone bearded figure, pick its way among the clutter of buildings and start to ride away.

Lamarie's hands were clenched and sweat broke out a second time that day as he wondered desperately if there was time, if the general could slip away without being discovered. How Texas had managed to persuade him Lamarie did not know, but she possessed a woman's witchery. For his part, he'd entertain and detain the invaders, to give him as long a start as possible.

And then, at first incredulously, a moment

late with unwilling understanding and admiration, he saw that the other rider was not keeping out of sight, but only appearing to try to do so; actually he was taking care to be glimpsed and recognized by the approaching column. Only when they spurred wildly in pursuit did he take off at a swinging gallop.

CHAPTER TEN

Appropriately, the town was named Randolph. It lay near the borders of the sprawling empire which made up Randolph Ranch, and for most of its existence the town had led a quiet, almost slumberous life. It was a cattle town, but it bore little relation to those towns of the plains country hundreds of miles to the north. Most of its buildings were adobe, heavy and substantial, cool at midday, warm at dawn. The few frame structures had aged and weathered so that they did not seem out of place.

There was a stone courthouse, likewise weathered and sleepy. It occupied one side of a square. Opposite it, beneath big trees, also a center of activity, stood a watering trough.

Cowboys came to town as occasion required, but they conducted themselves decorously. This was home, and to be treated as such. The natives even accorded a polite if distant welcome to the Yankees and carpetbaggers who were infiltrating the community. A few more of them arrived each month, unwelcome, but, like fleas, to be endured.

Dan Rather looked the town over with an appreciative eye as he rode in, doing so unobtrusively in the dusk of evening. His destination was another dozen miles beyond, but a dozen miles was no more than a whoop and a holler after the long trek by river and land.

Luck had been with him—the sort of fortune to which his troops had grown accustomed during the war years, the luck of Dan Rather. It was a tradition, akin to the song parody built about his name, that Dan Rather made his own luck. If he didn't like it, he was apt to take it by the seat of the pants and the scruff of the neck and either pitch it over the fence or scrub its face in a frying pan, until it was bright and acceptable.

Following the attack on the stage and the discovery of that fantastic ring, the trip had been relatively uneventful. The ring had been final proof of the duplicity of Planchette. However, Dan had left word at the next station, making sure that the fellow received a decent burial. When all was said and done, E. Planchette had had his points.

Dan allowed his horse to sink its muzzle in

the water of the trough, to drink slowly and allow the water to dribble past and around the bit, lazying a few moments, while the leaves of the big trees made a whisper overhead. Several other horses, saddled and bridled, cropped the thin remnants of grass nearby and cocked friendly ears toward them. There was no immediate sign of their riders.

Dan loitered also. Both of them had earned the moment of leisure. Presently he'd stable the horse, find a place to eat and enjoy a good meal, then seek out a bed. Tomorrow—

Tomorrow was a day to be savored even more than the meal or the bed at journey's end. His heart for some reason insisted on beating wildly, while schoolboy dreams flitted through his head, along with a wild quickening of his breath. Tomorrow he'd deliver the pardon into the hands of Texas Minifee, and hope to win a smile from those deep, serene eyes which each day had looked back at him out of the photo. And each time, they had seemed increasingly to gaze into his very heart.

It did no good to remind himself that this was a fanciful dream, and foolish; that she had signed herself, 'With all my love,' and sent the picture to John Marston, not to him. To Marston, who had been his rival, his enemy, and the victor over him, even if in winning he had lost. The twists and turns of life were as many and confusing as the trails in that often trackless land, and he should be old enough to know better than to dream.

He swung down from the saddle, his limbs stiff from long riding, and, kneeling, drank at the spout which poured a steady stream into the trough. Then he dipped his head under the cool water, swishing it back and forth, reveling in the wetness. Finally he brushed back his wet hair, got to his feet, and went cold at the pressure of a revolver's muzzle. It was thrust with a sudden hardness against the middle of his stomach.

Dismally he recognized that it was a proper punishment for relaxing his guard, even for a moment; he should have known better, now his destination was so close. But the square had seemed deserted, and he'd been certain that no one within a thousand miles had ever seen him or even heard of him.

He opened his eyes, brushing back the long dank hair, and stood still, looking about, conscious that no word had been spoken. There were five interlopers, tall men who stood silent and watchful, each holding a gun. The man who had jammed the gun against his middle was thoughtfully removing Dan's own revolver from its holster and transferring it to a pocket.

He was tall as Dan, and nearly of an age and build, only his hair and skin suggested a trace of Indian blood, and he'd had a haircut more recently. He was smiling—a

92

half-mocking, half-pleased smirk—leaning forward in the dusk to peer more sharply into Rather's face.

'So,' he nodded, 'Major Dan Rather in the flesh, is it not? You look as you were described to us, Major—and you arrive almost precisely on schedule. We were expecting you.'

The voice was courteously soft, but the gun muzzle was not. The grazing horses were explained. These men made up a reception committee, and they had probably loitered for hours or days in town. When he had dismounted, they had returned from a saloon or perhaps the shadows of the courthouse.

'So you're a reception committee,' Dan murmured. 'But not a welcoming one?'

White teeth flashed in a smile.

'You put it aptly, Mr. Rather. But do not mistake us. We are happy to see you, most pleased, since you carry that for which we have been waiting.'

Certain that he understood, Dan parried for time with an obvious question.

'I'm afraid that you have the advantage of me in more ways than one. And what might that be?'

Odds of five to one were always difficult, and now that they had his gun, yet still persisted in keeping their own guns trained, they could be fatal. Some of the horses had wandered closer, as though taking an interest in what went on.

Dan risked a backward step, bringing up with his back against one of the horses. It did not sidle away.

'I'd hear your story with more pleasure without that bit of steel boring into my belly,' he explained.

The spokesman remained unruffled, a smile lifting the edges of his mustache.

'Just as you wish, Major. You will, I hope, pardon the discourtesy, but we are aware of your reputation—and intend to take no chances. What we want is what you carry—the pardon for Randolph Minifee. And make no mistake, Mr. Rather. Hand it over and there will be no difficulty. Attempt even the slightest trick, and we'll kill you.'

The settling night was a pleasant cloak, the air softly scented. The moon made a faint gleam at the eastern rim of the horizon, showing that it would soon be looking down with an active interest. Until the light improved, the others would watch sharply.

Dan estimated his chances, and concluded that they had been fairly assessed. The odds in favor of anything save dying were too scant to merit consideration. On the other hand, it was certain that Texas would not smile upon him if he failed at this late date, and there was also the matter of pride.

The gloom was helpful, and his sense of touch, coupled with his earlier lazy survey, told him more. He was standing, his back to the rump of one of the horses. A pair of saddle bags were tied behind the saddle, hanging over on either side. He could feel one. Moreover, it appeared that the cover was unbuckled and hanging loose.

He thrust his head forward, lowering it, staring more intently.

'I suppose it's useless to suggest to you gentlemen that you have made a mistake—that I'm not the man you appear to be looking for, and that I certainly don't carry anything which could be of interest or value to anyone?'

'You're quite right, Major Rather—it would be useless to suggest it. Are you going to hand over that pardon, or must we be so rude as to search you?'

Dan sighed. Under cover of the gloom and the sudden thrust of his head, he could manage what could almost pass for sleight of hand. One arm, in their view, had not moved. But with the horse at his back, his other hand had dipped into an inner coat pocket and come out with a packet. Without turning, he had contrived to reach the saddle bag and drop it in. It was a temporary expedient and less than satisfactory, but preferable to the other alternative.

'If that's the way you feel, I suppose you'll have to search me, if only to satisfy yourselves that I'm telling the truth.' He sighed.

'Manifestly, I can't hand over something which I do not possess. But I must warn you, gentlemen—I shall consider such an indignity an insult.'

'Consider it and be damned,' was the brusque retort. Apparently the deepening darkness and his calm disclaimer were making them nervous. 'Since that's your choice, we'll have to search you. Lift your arms, and keep them up.'

A second time, but now from behind, a gun barrel was jammed against him, close above his heart. At the same moment he was seized and jerked roughly away from the horse. With the pressure of the revolver as a persuader, he stood quietly while they searched—doing a job which proclaimed them to be experts rather than amateurs.

They exclaimed softly at finding what they apparently wanted, but a swift examination convinced them that these were private papers and not the pardon. They found his derringer, also his money belt, but in one sense they were gentlemen. These they replaced, merely unloading the hand-gun. Then, with only his boots remaining, they insisted that he remove them.

Sitting on the ground, Dan complied. Only when they had satisfied themselves that he did not have any pardon on him did they come to an angry impasse.

'Blast it, you *must* be Dan Rather,' one man

protested. 'And you've *got* to have that pardon—'

'We're forgetting something,' a companion interjected. 'It must be on his horse.'

They turned eagerly to a search of the saddle, even stripping it off and probing the saddle blanket. Dan tugged his boots back on and stood waiting patiently.

'Well, gentlemen, I hope you're satisfied,' he said. 'If not—I don't quite see what's to be done.'

They were furious as well as baffled. Since there was obviously nowhere else to look, Dan shrugged.

'If you don't mind, I'm hungry and somewhat weary, and anxious to get some supper and a bed. But before I go, I warn you that I resent such cavalier treatment. So an apology is in order!'

'Go to the devil. You'll get no apology from us.'

'In that case—' Dan sighed, and moved with sudden swiftness as the light of the moon flooded the square. His fist lashed out, and the man who had prodded him with the revolver staggered back, then splashed full length into the horse trough.

CHAPTER ELEVEN

The spokesman for the five had named him; therefore it followed that they must also know him by reputation. But perhaps they had been deceived by the manner in which he had appeared to accept the inevitable, so that their vigilance had relaxed. Now they were given a demonstration of the man in action.

One of the others jumped to aid his leader, and made the mistake of trusting to his hands instead of his gun. He ended up on his back beside the watering trough, which was already occupied. Then Dan Rather had a pair of guns, and his voice rasped coldly.

'There are limits beyond which I permit no one to trespass with impunity. However, should you feel aggrieved, by all means take such action as pleases you—and which you are able to back!'

He awaited their reaction, and they waited, watching him, maintaining the silence which had marked the four from the first. The spokesman pulled himself half upright in the trough, then remained lolling like a Roman in his bath. Dan sighed.

'Since you have nothing more to add, this seems to conclude our business with one another. So I'll bid you a very good evening.'

The moon entangled itself in a taller tree,

bringing back deeper gloom. One took advantage of it, skulking like a phantom, making a dart and a leap for a saddle. The next instant he was gone, along with one of the horses. Dan choked on an icy lump rising in his throat, his eyes searching the gloom. Four of the ponies remained, and he had taken note of all of them as he rode in. None of these was the animal against which he had leaned, and even in the darkness he could make out the humped back of the saddles, none with the betraying bulge of saddle bags behind. Whether by mischance or intention, that one was gone.

Dan reached his own horse and followed, fighting an impulse to spur, his ears adjusted for sounds from ahead. They assured him that the escaping man was not hastening, well aware that swift hoofs would sound loud in the night. Dan held grimly to his own pace, hoping to glimpse him when the moonlight flooded back, to remedy what had taken on the aspect of a mocking jest.

He could have no sure answer to the vital question. Had the fellow witnessed or at least guessed at his deft transfer of the papers to the saddle bags, then seized the first opportunity to make off with the horse? The possibility was tormenting.

Yet the weight of evidence was against such a possibility. If any of them had noticed what he was about, they would have acted promptly, since their guns had been on him and it was the papers they desired, not himself. But such thoughts were academic; recovering the pardon was of first importance.

Even an owl's eyes would hardly see around a corner, and apparently the horse and rider had turned one. Dan reflected on what he had been able to see. The saddle was ornately carved, and he'd made certain which one it was by the sense of touch, even with his back turned. The horse, which had appeared ghostly in the gloom, was a roan, its left hind foot white. The brand on its hip had been a Diamond J, though the other horses had worn a Lone Star above the half-circle of a moon. The Diamond J resembled a fishhook, and the scar of the brand had shown gray against the darker hair of the flank.

It was little enough to go on, should he lose track of the horse before recovering the pardon. And if the rider by mischance should look to see what the saddle bag contained—

Apparently the others were not attempting to follow, at least not with any haste. He swung around a darkly looming building, which from the odor was a barn, and a horseman was ahead. The cayuse could be a roan, but the distance and light were deceptive, and luck chose that moment to play a prank.

Half a dozen riders came galloping into town from a side road, sweeping up, engulfing the lone horseman. They shouted greetings as they recognized him, and Dan made out the name, Sandy. Then they were across and onto a side street, out of sight, the sound of hoofs muted abruptly. By the time he reached the intersection, the street lay empty under the moon.

At least it was empty of riders. This was the business section, and a score of horses were lined along hitch rails; dismounted men were tying steeds, then clumping across a boardwalk, their spurs making a faint jingle in contrast to the thump of high heels. A swinging door opened and closed, its light revealing only a tangle of legs. Silence came back as the door was shut, and a horse at the rack sighed gustily.

Dan selected a tree at the opposite side of the street, and tied his horse in the blanketing shadow. Then he walked softly in the dust, surveying each horse from behind. He frowned in disbelief as he reached the end of the line and retraced his steps, examining each animal more closely. But there was no roan, no pair of saddle bags.

It jolted him. He'd been confident, sure that he was right—but somewhere, covered by the confusion and the darkness, the man on the road had dodged into an alley or behind a shed and vanished.

The implications were shattering. To bring the pardon this far, only to lose it, was a blow to his ego; the further consequences were unthinkable. It was a bad dream, and unless he did something about it, the dream would turn into a nightmare.

It had seemed too good an opportunity to miss, to use the handy receptacle afforded by the saddle bag, in that instant when discovery had been imminent. Now, regrets for what might have been were useless. He climbed back into his saddle and made a patient circle of the town, back and forth, along each deserted street. Yellow light made fugitive gleams in a score of shaded windows, but the only night life of the town seemed to center in the one saloon. He found a few additional ponies, patiently awaiting the pleasure of their masters, but none was the horse he sought.

Returning finally to the barn, he swung down, routing out a sleepy stable boy, helping him care for his horse. In the process he checked the occupied stalls, again making certain that the roan was not in one. When he returned to the street he was forced to confess himself at a loss, a man without a plan.

It would be easy to read at least suspicion into the action of the man who had taken the roan and so abruptly deserted his fellows, and the possibility that he had guessed the hiding place of the paper was disturbing. Still he might have been eager to get away and report to whoever had hired them for that job—to report that Dan Rather had come to town, and that they had failed to find what they were after.

Since that possibility existed, he still had a chance. If the pardon had already been found, he had lost. If not, there was still hope. The saddle bags might go for days or weeks unused, without being looked into. If that happened, there was the chance he might find them again.

It was hardly a set of odds to please a gambler; still, he'd faced long odds before. He slipped into the saloon, finding, as he had hoped, that they ran an eating place in conjunction with it. None of the customers was familiar. In turn, no one paid much attention to him. Strangers were increasingly common, and, if scarcely welcome, they were endured.

The bartender, who doubled as a waiter, nodded and jerked a thumb. Sleeping rooms were available above the saloon, reached by an outside stairs. The accommodations might have been worse. Already, the bar below and the town was quieting, as the last customers drifted out and allowed their horses to head home with them.

One among Rather's guesses was accurate. Sandy Blair had acted both on impulse and on orders, making a break when he saw a chance, getting onto the nearest horse and riding. Instructions from the boss had been pointed and particular.

'Shorty'll more or less appoint himself to be in charge, of course—he always does,' the boss had observed. 'That's all right—only I want to be able to check up on him, to know how things are going, 'special if anything goes wrong. You see to that, Sandy.'

It was almost a pleasure to obey, even though he was the bearer of bad news. Shorty Landrum's assumption of authority and superiority had become almost unbearable, and Sandy was eager to report how the matter had been bungled. Leaving the town behind, he rode fast.

Some of his eagerness ebbed as he approached his destination and remembered the unpredictable temper of his employer. But by now he was in for it. Having ridden ahead, he had to report.

Tilbury Jenkins, awakened from a sound sleep, stared bleary-eyed. He'd fortified himself against the normal disappointments of the day with the usual libations of the evening, tipping the bottle in the privacy of his own house; an extra one for some vaguely mysterious road left him in a fuzzy state as he awakened.

He listened as his henchman reported, incredulity giving way to anger. Vaguely he associated the latter with the bearer of unpleasant tidings. It was bad enough to be awakened at all, without hearing such a message.

'Are you tryin' to tell me that Dan Rather rode into town—and *didn't* have that pardon on him?' he demanded. 'You're crazy. He had to have it.'

'All I know is that he didn't,' Sandy retorted stubbornly. He was not a redhead for nothing. 'We searched him—made him take off his boots, everything. He said he didn't have it, and he didn't.'

'So he made a fool of you,' Tilbury observed acidly. 'I might have known I shouldn't send a set of fools to do a job. But what's a man to do, when that's all he has to work with? What happened then?'

Sandy told him, relishing relating the part where Landrum had been deposited in the horse trough. At that juncture, he had made good his escape.

Tilbury listened sourly, attempting in his fuzzy-minded state to assess the consequences. That was not easy, but the more he considered, the more appalled he became. For months now, ever since he'd heard about John Marston and his success in wangling a pardon for Randolph Minifee from Abe Lincoln, he'd been gambling, playing for big stakes. Hiring an array of messengers, some former acquaintances, despatching instructions and money by mail had already cost him a pretty penny; so much that he was teetering on the brink of bankruptcy.

But Randolph Ranch, with Texas Minifee thrown in, was worth gambling for. Moreover, wasn't he the proper, the logical heir, being the only blood kin of the general, aside from Texas? The kinship had been a ranking aggravation for as long as he could remember. Wasn't blood thicker than water? That being so, wasn't it the plain duty of the general to treat him as kin folks? And what should that mean, but to be accepted as one of the family, given at least the foremanship of Randolph Ranch, the hand of Texas in marriage, and all that would normally be implied?

Instead, he was received with civility but never with cordiality, and had he not been kin, however distant, he had long since recognized that he'd have been given the boot. Those were wrongs over which he had brooded long, then had set out to remedy them as opportunity beckoned.

Possession of that presidential pardon was the key. With it, he would hold the general's life and honor in his hands, and his price would be acceptance as a son and heir. Whatever the cost, the prize was worth it.

He'd soldiered with McHugh and Lamont, and since the war they had kept in touch. Both were scoundrels, completely untrustworthy, except that they'd do anything for the promise of a proper reward. And that he had been able to dangle before their eyes.

Everything had appeared to be working perfectly, until Dan Rather had somehow become involved. And now—

Tilbury Jenkins came suddenly to his feet from the edge of the bed, screaming in a frenzy of frustration. Dan Rather had gotten as far as the borders of Randolph Ranch, and he'd flummoxed the five, even after they'd had the drop on him. Which meant, of course, that he still had the pardon, and tomorrow he'd turn it over either to Texas or the general; and with that, all his hopes would go glimmering. It was too much.

'You're an idiot,' he shouted, 'a bungling donkey, you and the whole pack of fools I sent to do a job! If you couldn't find that paper on him, why couldn't you tie him up and bring him to me? Instead of that you let him get away, and then you come squalling to me about how you've failed!'

'Get out,' he added. 'Get on your horse and ride—clear out of the country! If I ever set eyes on you again, I won't be responsible for what I'll do. I can't stand the sight of such stupid loons! Get out, before I lose my temper!'

CHAPTER TWELVE

Dutifully but not expectantly, Dan made another round of the town by daylight. The horses which had cluttered the hitch rails were gone, and no new ones had taken their places. For once, possessing a tongue was scarcely an asset, since he dared ask no questions. Even to mention the roan horse and its brand would be to focus attention upon it, and any chance which might remain would be lost.

So far, there was no stir of excitement. He suspected that if the pardon fell into the hands of those who sought it, violent repercussions would follow swiftly. But it was too soon for the quiet to be encouraging.

His destination had been Randolph Ranch, but there seemed little point in going there if he could report no better than failure. Inquiry revealed that a smaller, neighboring ranch to the Randolph owned the brand variously known as Diamond J, the Swinging J or the Fishhook. It was owned by Tilbury Jenkins.

The name meant nothing, but a Diamond J horse might well be found on its own outfit.

He left the trace behind, deliberately turning off where the road dwindled to trails through the grass. Topping a slope, he studied a panorama of partly wooded valley and partly open meadow. Scrub oak abounded, and the aspect was as primitive as on the day when Texas had first raised its own flag to the breeze, the lone star at once a challenge and a promise.

He started to ride on, then hesitated, drawing presently to the cover of a clump of trees, as sound flung itself ahead of a galloping horse. The cayuse burst into sight down and part way across the valley, heading toward him. On that course, it would pass not far from where he sat. Dan observed what was happening with a quickening pulse, stirred as always by a chase.

The rider came on, glancing back over his shoulder, and the cause of his uneasiness was apparent as other horsemen came into view; there were at least half a dozen, men who spurred and quirted their horses in a desperate effort to narrow the gap.

The pursued was a man with long full beard, and even at that distance there seemed something vaguely familiar about him. Clothe him in a uniform, say that of a ranking officer of the Confederacy, and the scene would take on added familiarity—

Furthermore, those who pursued were in the blue uniform of the United States cavalry.

Only one thing was missing. There was no shooting. They were making no effort to down the fugitive with their rifles. That was probably because they hoped to take him alive, and were confident of their ability to do so within the next few minutes.

The fugitive could scarcely be other than Randolph Minifee, the general himself. That would account for everything, including their wish to take him alive and unharmed.

Dan Rather took note of several factors. Most significant, the fleeing horse was running poorly, as though the chase had been a long one; also, it appeared to be limping, as if from an injury. Unless something were done, and quickly, the chase could have only one conclusion.

This was the moment when he should have ridden triumphantly into view, to halt both pursued and pursuer with a gesture, to produce the pardon and dumbfound the Yankees.

No such heroics being possible, he considered what might be done. Shooting from ambush, he could severely decimate the ranks of the pursuers before they even suspected danger, and thus assure the escape of Minifee. But that seemed somewhat drastic. The war was over. True, they had placed his name on the proscribed list, along with that of Randolph Minifee, John Marston, and many others. But even that was hardly reason enough to put himself forever beyond the bounds of hope or pardon, and in the class with common murderers.

Still, something had to be contrived, and

soon, or it would be too late.

His roving glance paused, focusing sharply. Sometime in the gloom of night he'd been fooled, but this was daylight, and his eyes were keen. A smile tightened his mouth even as it relaxed its grimness. Here was a perverse piece of luck, which might be turned to good account.

At least it would do no harm to try, even if he failed—as was possible, since the object might be old and possibly untenanted. It was a dull gray, and it blended with the green of the tree and the branch from which it was suspended. Its obvious state of repair argued against desertion, and he lifted his revolver as the fugitive passed almost under the tree and went on, never guessing what was so close above.

It would be a long shot for a forty-five, but possible. The general was swiftly out of sight, the blue-clad riders sweeping close. Dan squeezed the trigger.

He saw the swift, startled reaction at the sound of the gun, the questing glances as they wondered where the shot had come from, and if they might be the target. Then they lost interest in such abstract questions, being suddenly confronted with a matter of more striking force. Hornets came pouring wrathfully from their suddenly violated nest and, seeing a horde of blue-clad invaders

111

passing directly below, swept vengefully at them.

CHAPTER THIRTEEN

Warily, Dan watched the devastation he had unleashed, punching out the empty shell and replacing it with a fresh cartridge before returning the gun to its holster. Until the evening before, the revolver had not been his property, but from the way it shot it seemed a fair trade.

Pandemonium was a wild word, but only mildly expressive of what was taking place. When they felt that they were aggrieved, or that their privacy had been invaded, the stubby little insects had a direct method of retaliation; nor did they stop to question or ascertain reasons or causes. They drove like bullets at men and horses, stinging, indiscriminately, and the chase ended as a new one was begun. The horses fled madly, encouraged by their riders still pursued by a scattering cloud of avengers.

Uneasy peace returned to the valley. Men and horses were gone, but an angry hum denoted that enough of the enraged insects had remained in the vicinity or were returning to make it a place to shun. He swung in a wide circle, to reach the trail taken by Minifee.

The fugitive would have heard the shot, so there seemed a good chance that he would have pulled up, either to watch or to rest his horse. Having nothing better in mind, Rather decided that it would be well to consult with him, even if that meant confessing his failure. Minifee, as the principal and the man most concerned in all this, had a right to know. He might be able to give some helpful advice.

The sun lay warm and bright on the slope beyond. Somewhere a bird essayed a tentative note, breaking the silence which had followed the gun shot and the terror unleashed by it. Dan felt sorry for the unhappy victims, who had only been doing their duty. Nonetheless, he grinned at the recollection. In checking them at so crucial a moment, he had given a measure of atonement for his earlier failure—

His horse gave an uneasy snort; then he saw what had disturbed it and rode quickly forward.

Minifee lay sprawled on the ground, unmoving. Dan could only guess at what had occurred; the likeliest answer was that at least one of the maddened hornets had pursued him, launching its own attack. Probably the horse had bucked wildly, throwing its rider. No longer plagued by the insect and over its fright, the pony was beginning to graze not far away.

This was enemy country; the faint buzz of the still furious insects came clearly though a rise of wooded ground separated the nest from that spot. Discreetly, Dan left his horse at a distance and moved stealthily on foot.

Reaching the fallen man, he dropped to his knees, frowning, at a loss. The heavy black beard was as luxuriant as whiskers could manage, but something was not quite right. The fair whiteness of the skin above, the long eyelashes against the pallid face—

The general seemed slighter than he had supposed, but for the moment that was an advantage. Dan stooped and picked him up. He'd glimpsed a stream not too far ahead, and water should be a restorative. Taking a step, he stopped, his breath catching sharply.

The whiskers at first had appeared to be disordered, but now he saw that they had slipped enough to reveal their falseness. It came to him that it was not a man cradled in his arms, but a woman.

At that instant the eyelids fluttered open, accompanied by a sigh. Eyes deeply blue but momentarily vacant looked into his, then widened in sudden amazement. There were other emotions, a riot of feeling which flowed and stormed through her eyes, running the gamut from bewilderment to recognition and a swift-mounting rage.

For all the concealing whiskers, he recognized her in turn and all but dropped her. Not only did he hold a woman in his arms, but this was the one woman, she who had filled his dreams, waking or sleeping, during the last weeks. What he'd dreamed of had come true, and Texas was in his arms.

'Put me down!' Her voice was a trifle unsteady, but the tone blazed. 'At once!'

Dan obeyed not too reluctantly, since her proximity seemed without reason to have turned his flesh to jelly, setting even his bones to quivering. He lowered her, steadying her with one hand as she swayed and seemed in danger of collapse. Instinctively she clutched at his protective arm, white teeth biting furiously on a red lip; then fury came to her rescue, and she shook loose his arm.

The next moment, surprisingly swift, she jerked a derringer and thrust it into his face.

'Hand over that pardon, Dan Rather, or I'll kill you!' she warned.

Dan watched her, bemused, his eyes ranging along the twin barrels of the gun to the pair of eyes blazing behind it. The gun itself made far less impression on him than the girl. Many times, events had moved at almost catastrophic speed, and as an officer, forced to make swift decisions, he had grown accustomed to taking events in stride. But this was beyond anything in his experience.

'Texas!' he breathed. 'I never guessed you could be so pretty!'

'Pretty!' She glared at him, disconcerted, amazed, still furious. 'Pretty! In *these* things!' She tore at the whiskers with her free hand, ripping them away, wincing as the paste with which they had been applied resisted so abrupt a divorce from so pretty a face, to which they seemed sensibly to cling. 'Are you crazy?'

He shook his head, still feasting his eyes on her, not quite certain any of this was happening. With the masking beard off, she was indubitably the Texas of the photograph, even prettier than the art of a master photographer could capture. The realization that it was she he had saved from capture left him dazed and bewildered.

'Crazy?' he repeated. 'No, I guess not. Mostly I'm surprised. I sure didn't guess that it was *you* those Yankees were chasing!'

It was Texas' turn to look bewildered. She glanced hastily around, as though suddenly remembering the chase. 'What—where are they?' she asked. 'I don't seem to remember—'

'They're gone,' he assured her. 'At the rate they took off, they'll be miles from here by now. Your horse must have thrown you somehow. Likely you were dazed—'

Texas lifted the fingers of her free hand, to feel tentatively of a lump at the back of her head, which was swelling to noticeable proportions, and was undoubtedly tender to the touch. She eyed him uncertainly, then, as if noticing the weapon in her hand for the first time, seemed at a loss as to what to do with it.

Some of her anger blazed back.

'I want that pardon!' she repeated. 'Now!'

'Or you'll shoot me?' he added, and grinned. 'That seems to be sort of a habit with folks here in Texas. A bunch of fellows said the same thing to me no longer ago than last evening.'

Texas' eyes widened. She had recognized Dan Rather instantly, having seen a tintype of him in uniform, when visiting her father during the course of the war. But somehow he was not like the picture, not at all as she had come to think of him in her mind. Here was the Dan Rather of song and tradition, of myth—but not the *old* Dan Rather of advanced, even decrepit years. It came to her almost as a shock that he didn't look a day older than in the tintype, that the picture must have been a recent instead of a youthful one—although it was that as well. Confused, she glimpsed the lurking grin in the back of his eyes, as though he could read her thoughts. It both charmed and infuriated her.

'What do you mean?' she demanded.

Dan shook his head ruefully.

'Since I've found you, Miss Texas, I might as well tell the truth and have it over with,' he decided. 'Back on the river Colonel Marston asked me, in case anything should happen to him, to bring that pardon to you—and to give it either to your father or into your own hands. So I set out to try. And I got as far as

117

town, last night—and lost it.'

The barrels of the little gun wavered, and she did not even notice. Her face went suddenly pale again, the returning trace of color swallowed in dismay.

'You lost it?' she whispered.

He nodded glumly.

'Lost or misplaced, it's gone, and I'm downright disgusted with myself,' he confessed. He recounted what had happened as briefly and clearly as possible. Her eyes remained fixed on his face, and she did not interrupt. Then, again discovering the gun in her hand, she colored. Hastily she returned it to its hiding place.

'That's what happened. I'm not proud of my part in it, though at the time it seemed a reasonable notion. But I'm hopeful that the pardon's still in that pair of saddle bags, and that it can be found again—before somebody else discovers it!' He added, on a note of such sincerity that she could not doubt him:

'It's not so much that I mind making a bad mistake myself, though I don't like that, or even letting Marston down, after I gave him my word. That's bad enough. But I aimed to place that pardon in your hands, Miss Texas—and I'd do almost anything to manage that now, for your sake as much as your father's.'

At the intensity of his words, color swirled through her cheeks in a sudden rush and her eyes dropped. Then she looked up again, confused but sober.

'I'm afraid I owe you an apology, Dan Rather,' she confessed. 'I seem to have misjudged you—gravely. Now I have a feeling that you are telling the truth.'

'Miss Texas,' he said earnestly. 'I've been accused of a lot of things, one time and another, and some of them with plenty of justification. But I've never been called a liar. I—well, I'll tell you something else. When he asked me to deliver that pardon to you, in case anything prevented him from doing so, Colonel Marston showed me your picture. I—it did something to me. It was like looking at you, right into your face, and as if you were looking at me, trusting me. I made up my mind that I'd do it for you—or die trying!'

Her breath caught again at the feeling in his words, the light in his eyes. She clutched at a minor phrase.

'My picture?' she repeated. 'How—Colonel Marston had it?'

Dan's eyes clouded. His nod was sober.

'The one where you'd written, "With all my love." I was bringing it back to you along with the pardon, till it was lost last night, being in the same envelope.'

She eyed him strangely, but her doubts had been removed. Tilbury Jenkins had been mistaken—that at least. Beyond the peradventure of a doubt, she knew which man she would believe.

When she spoke again, she was characteristically decisive.

'In that case, we've got to plan how to find the pardon before anyone else does,' she agreed. 'I've done you an injustice, and I do apologize and ask your pardon. You see—I was told that Colonel Marston had been murdered and the pardon stolen from him by a man named Dan Rather! Also that you were heading this way, and would use the pardon to try to blackmail me!'

Dan nodded understandingly.

'That makes sense,' he conceded. 'There's been a lot of scheming going on around that piece of paper, and I can guess at some of the reasons. But who knows so much about me and my whereabouts as to say all those things?'

Texas' eyes darkened as she considered that angle. Again her nod was decisive.

'I was told all that by Tilbury Jenkins,' she admitted. 'He's my cousin. I don't know just how he got the information ahead of your arrival, but apparently he managed. Naturally, he's concerned for my welfare and that of Randolph Ranch, as well as my father's. But someone must have gotten a lot of things garbled.'

'It sounds that way,' Dan agreed. 'And now, would you mind telling me what you were doing, disguised to look like your father, and being chased by Yankee soldiers?'

Texas colored, glancing down at her attire with sudden embarrassment.

'Father was in a riding accident today,' she explained. 'He broke a leg—so he is laid up. I learned that a detachment of soldiers, led by a Captain Culdeen, were coming to arrest him. I had made plans for such a possibility, so I clapped on those whiskers and rode off, allowing myself to be seen.'

'And chased.' Dan nodded. 'You took a big chance.'

'What else was there to do?' she countered. 'I'd have been all right—I could lead them around and lose them anywhere, anytime I chose. Only my horse slipped on a round stone and went lame. After that I was having a hard time—until you came to my assistance.'

'That way, eh? We've delayed them—but now they'll be twice as determined. Do you have any notion about the Diamond J brand?'

Again her eyes darkened, but her answer, as always, was straightforward.

'Yes. Diamond J belongs to Tilbury Jenkins.'

CHAPTER FOURTEEN

Excitement was in the air, throbbing in his veins, and it sprang from more than the wildness of the chase or the savagery of the hornets. It bubbled like the waters in a hot spring, exhilarating, potent. Dan Rather had a giddy sensation that he was a boy again, that he'd reached Texas at last—the real Texas, beyond which a man need look no farther.

He was foolish, and he didn't even care. These other bits and pieces of news were interesting, but they had lost the power to surprise.

'You had better come along home and meet my father,' Texas decided. 'He'll want to see you, and we can talk things over with him. He's long been an admirer of yours,' she added frankly. 'I was, too, until I was regaled with a whole book of horror stories about you. Now I know that those weren't so—and it leaves me wondering why they were told.'

'It sounds to me as though we're like a couple of robins,' Dan suggested: 'a pair that have been tugging at opposite ends of an angleworm at the same time, without suspecting how much is still in the ground. I'm beginning to realize that we're involved in a well-planned thing, I'm curious as to how all this about me reached here before I could arrive. I've been traveling as fast as I could manage. There must have been a spy system, operating efficiently long before I boarded the *Mississippi Belle*. But I didn't notice any telegraph wires into town.'

'There is none,' Texas agreed. 'But there is a wire from St. Louis to Big Springs. A man with a fast horse, operating between here and there, could keep someone pretty well posted.' She clapped a hand to her mouth, eyeing him strangely. 'And I know that Tilbury has made a couple of trips to Big Springs lately, besides sending some of his men back and forth. But it couldn't be Tilbury. He—it just couldn't.'

'Why not?' Dan demanded. 'Doesn't he fit the picture in other ways?'

Her face was gravely thoughtful. 'Well—now you've set me to wondering! He's a relation—sort of—and he wants to marry me—which he should know I wouldn't even consider—' Her eyes narrowed still further.

'It sounds impossible, but only because he's too dumb. It just doesn't fit.'

'Looks can be deceptive,' Dan reminded her.

Meanwhile Randolph Minifee was submitting as gracefully as possible to the indignity of lying in bed, but he was utilizing otherwise wasted time according to his own notions. He was sitting, propped up by pillows, his splinted leg stretched before him, a score of books scattered on the bed within reach. His scholarly ambitions were constantly being stifled by the lack of time to pursue them. Mere discomfort he dismissed as no hindrance.

He glanced up, eyeing Texas keenly, then placed a finger in his book to mark his place. His eyes strayed to Dan, and surprise, mixed with uncertainty, came into them. The bewilderment was as quickly followed by a flare of excitement.

'Don't tell me!' he commanded. 'I should know you, sir—I have a conviction that I do. But you're new in Texas!'

Dan nodded, while Texas watched with resigned exasperation. Her father should have been asleep, or at least resting quietly, but she was resigned to his conduct. A broken bone could knit as well by itself as if sympathy were wasted upon it. Randolph Minifee could be gentle as a woman in pitying the ills of others, but he wasted no pity on himself.

'Why, yes, General, I am new in Texas,' Dan admitted. 'It's a far piece from the Shenandoah.'

'The Shenadoah?' Minifee repeated; then his brow cleared. Disregarding his place in the book, he allowed it to fall to the floor, while he leaned forward to extend his hand.

'Of course! You soldiered there in '63—and to such good purpose that everybody started

124

to sing a song about you! I've been rather jealous of that song, Dan Rather, to say nothing of the man. But welcome to Texas.'

Dan gripped the hand warmly. Texas, watching, was surprised as well as pleased to see that he was embarrassed.

'The song was about the wrong man, General.'

'Not for a moment! As to recognizing you, I saw a tintype of you once. You're better-looking than it was. But what brings you to Texas, Dan?'

Texas answered that. 'You, Dad!'

Minifee looked surprised. 'Me? Ridiculous. The war's over, and with it, any importance I may ever have had.'

'I was bringing your pardon, from Abraham Lincoln,' Dan explained. 'Only I've lost it.'

'You were actually bringing such an instrument? From Mr. Lincoln? I've been inclined to believe that the whole tale was a fabrication.'

'It was real enough. Only last night I lost it.'

'Wade Hampton told me once that you were too honest for your own good! How could you lose what you weren't supposed to possess? My understanding was that it was being carried here by that scoundrel of a Marston!'

At the epithet, Dan blinked incredulously.

There had been no love lost between the colonel and himself, but he had assumed there was a close friendship with this family, and Texas in particular. Texas protested.

'Oh, but, Dad, Colonel Marston *did* interest himself and obtain the pardon—'

'So he says! Not that I doubt it, for I wouldn't put it past him. He was always an opportunist as well as a scoundrel, and doing such a thing would offer him a chance to place us under obligation. He made a good officer,' he added grudgingly. 'But as a man, he had no scruples.'

'He's dead, Dad,' Texas protested.

'That's why I'm curbing my tongue to speak only good of the devil,' Minifee growled. His glance lingered on his daughter, and his eyes grew hooded. Then he swung back to Dan. 'Whatever may have happened, you're still welcome in Texas and on Randolph Ranch, Dan Rather,' he said. 'But I take it that you have a story to tell?'

He listened attentively while Dan recounted what he considered important, and Texas filled in with certain details. At the story of the hornets, he grinned broadly.

'The sting of those insects can be as uncharitable as my thoughts,' he observed. 'Still, it served the Yankees right. But you took a big chance, girl, riding in such fashion. You knew I wouldn't approve.'

Texas nodded serenely. 'That's why I
126

didn't ask you.'

Minifee grimaced, spread his hands, then smiled. 'You see what I'm up against, Dan, she on one side, and the Yankees on the other? And she won't concede that I'm old enough to look out for myself.'

'You didn't do too good a job today,' Texas pointed out, 'though I'll concede that the spill which you took was no accident.' She went on to recount how she had found the burr under the saddle, and what had subsequently happened.

'You say that Javits was shot just as he was about to talk?' Minifee repeated incredulously. 'Why, this thing is more serious than I had supposed. I didn't realize that we harbored traitors on Randolph Ranch.'

'With you dead, the ranch would be a rich booty,' Dan pointed out. 'And that is a notion which apparently has occurred to a good many people.'

'You've been too good an evangelist, Dad,' Texas chided him. 'When everyone else was weeping and moaning, you've gone around assuring them that Texas and the whole country still has a future, that it won't be long until we'll be so prosperous that we'll forget we ever were poor.'

'Well, what's wrong about bragging, as long as it isn't about yourself?' Minifee countered. 'I have tried to put a fighting spirit into some of our people,' he explained to Dan. 'Too many of them have figured that we were not only broke, but down and out, with a horde of carpetbaggers swarming in to exploit us, so that nothing could ever be right again. Of course things are bad. There are cattle running everywhere, and no market. The country has been devastated by war, so that even the North is almost bankrupt. But there's one star in the sky, and while it may be small, it will be like the lean kine of Egypt which ate up all the fat cows—and will outshine all the rest of the constellation one of these days.

'I'm talking about the Homestead Act. Even if I'd hated him for everything else, I'd love Abe Lincoln for signing that! There are tens of thousands of dirt-poor people who'll be moving west to better themselves—or more likely millions. It will take time, but one of these days the wilderness will blossom, and cattle will mean wealth. Anyhow, that's what I've been saying.'

Dan nodded agreement. 'I'd go along with you on that, suh. And when that day comes, Randolph Ranch will be a ready-made empire—and only *you* will stand in the way of someone taking it over!'

'That's where you're wrong. Anybody who underestimates Texas the lady is as foolish as those who belittle Texas the state. But of course you're right, about my being in their way.'

'Which brings us to the question of what to do next,' Dan said, 'especially in view of my bungling.'

'I wouldn't call it by so harsh a word, and I'm not sure but what I'm glad that the pardon's lost. If I could be certain that it wouldn't turn up again, I would be. It was planned as a weapon to be used against us, as you've pointed out, and not as a gift. And it could be a nasty sort of club.'

On that point there was no question. Possession of the pardon could involve Texas in the struggle as deeply as her father. Not only did she love her father, but she was heir to Randolph Ranch, as well as being young and desirable.

The general relaxed suddenly, sinking back among the pillows, white and drawn. Man of iron though he was, there was a limit to what the flesh could take.

'If the ranch and Texas weren't mixed up in this, I'd say let them take me, and willingly.' He sighed. 'Sometimes the game's not worth the candle. Still, with you here, Dan, I'm not worrying. Let the other side do that! I'll just turn over and go to sleep, and quit feeling sorry for them!'

Determinedly, he turned and closed his eyes. Dan encountered Texas' gaze, which widened to a smile as she led the way from the room.

'You know, Dan, I think he's right,' she said softly.

From widely separated points, two men had watched the meeting between Dan and Texas following her mishap. One was Rab Culdeen, captain of cavalry, U.S. Army. Somewhere along the way of the years he had left his swagger behind, even though he was a man entitled to swagger.

Culdeen looked upon himself as a patient man and long-suffering—especially the latter, since the assignment to track down and arrest Randolph Minifee was a task which his compatriots had declared might be impossible as well as distasteful. If Minifee was a legend in the South, he was a hero in his own state and Texans were notoriously touchy in regard to the molestation of household idols. Nor were they so long or far removed from treason and violence as to regard a little more of the same as unreasonable.

Upon receiving his orders, to proceed to Texas and ferret out the owner of Randolph Ranch, Culdeen had reflected that the peacetime pursuits of a soldier could be very nearly as unpleasant as war. But a man did not argue with orders; he obeyed.

Randolph Ranch was an empire in itself, almost as huge in its way as the mighty state of which it was a part. The town of Randolph lay along one corner of its southern rim, and there were other towns whose sole reason for being was the ranch.

Culdeen had learned something of its size and complexity for himself. Over a period of weeks, patiently following rumors, clues and reports, he had ridden widely, seeking but never finding a man as elusive as mist. Well aware that many of the tales were probably prepared especially for his ears, that his chase was like pursuit of the winging wild goose, and that everyone in that part of Texas was laughing at him, Rab Culdeen had remained unperturbed. This was part of the exercise of patience and he had not been illpleased.

There were reasons, some of them as complex as the man. He was in no hurry. His superiors expected the job to be a slow one, and he saw no reason to expedite a distasteful duty. To fight an enemy in open warfare was one thing; taking vengeance upon the vanquished left a dark taste upon the tongue.

He did not mind the covert laughter; these people had few enough pleasures, so why deny them a few jibes at a simple-minded Yankee. Besides being enjoyable as well as time-consuming, his rides brought an increasing familiarity with the country. Knowledge of the terrain might prove useful.

His third reason was purely personal— nothing less than a secret admiration for Randolph Minifee. The owner of Randolph Ranch had been a brave, resourceful leader in war, gentlemanly, generous to captive foes.

Rab Culdeen had a brother, now alive, who but for that might as easily have been dead.

But at last he was being pressed for action. So that day Culdeen had set out, with a score of men at his heels, making a positive if tentative move.

Riding down the long avenue of trees, approaching the ranch buildings, they had witnessed the hurried leave-taking of their quarry and had swung in pursuit. It had occurred to Rab Culdeen that this might prove an interesting chase, playing hounds to such a fox.

The next hours had abundantly confirmed that opinion. Wryly, he reached the conclusion that he still had much to learn about the country, and the best ways of getting over it. It took only a few minutes to convince him that the black-bearded rider was playing with them. Here was a horseman who knew every trail and path, every hill and gulch, stream or patch of brush, and who could appear to take chances, then cause his pursuers to look ridiculous.

Culdeen was not displeased. He intended to do his best, but he was in no hurry to end the game. It soon became apparent that any chance of doing so was slimmer than he had thought. Within an hour, his force had been halved, as the pace grew hotter and many of his men were unable to keep up. Some, striking off at angles in an effort to head off the fugitive, had only gotten lost.

But luck had a way of scattering favors, first to one side, then to the other. Now it was with them. The horseman ahead was slowing, his steed suddenly gone lame.

Culdeen could find no heart to rejoice at such a turn of events. But as a soldier, he could not refuse to pursue the advantage. He called upon his horse, and upon himself and those who still rode with him, for a final spurt—and rode straight into torment.

The enraged hornets struck viciously and without warning. When his fleeing horsemen had finally outdistanced the live missiles, Culdeen had taken stock.

For himself, he had been twice lucky, once in that he had been stung only a couple of times, again in that he was less susceptible to stings than most people. Most of his men were in bad shape, with swollen hands and faces. Some had been thrown by maddened horses, and all were in need of rest and healing. His forces were well scattered.

Instructing his lieutenant to round up the stragglers and head back to town, Culdeen circled, curious to discover, if possible, just what had happened, and how. It seemed obvious that Minifee had not deliberately led them into that trap, or fired the shot which had triggered the hornets' wrath. That had been clever strategy, but someone else had been involved.

From a distance, he watched while Dan Rather worked to restore the fallen Minifee to consciousness, then shook his head in wry admiration as he saw the false beard twitched aside and realized that it was a woman who had bamboozled them so completely.

Now this Culdeen decided, will take some looking into. And who is this new actor who comes thus upon the scene, to our discomfort? One thing sure, he added, you've better luck than you deserve, mister. And what wouldn't I give to be in your boots?

CHAPTER FIFTEEN

From a point nearly opposite, about half a mile away, Tilbury Jenkins also watched the encounter, doing so with considerably less detachment than did the Yankee captain. Tilbury had been on his way back to his own ranch, following a roundabout course for reasons which he considered good. It would be troublesome and might prove embarrassing, should he be asked to explain why he had been hanging around the buildings on Randolph Ranch, long after he had publicly departed.

Acquainted as he was with every old building and rabbit-run around, it had not been too difficult to linger on, so as to reassure Javits that he had nothing to fear. The door lock had hardly snapped shut on him before Jenkins was opening it again, counseling him to a course of silence, promising him an adequate reward for doing so.

Thoughtfully, Tilbury had left the door unlocked, so that Javits could avoid any questions which might prove hard to answer. He had been on the point of a second departure when Texas had displayed such a shockingly good example of marksmanship, bringing down Javits' horse, cutting off his escape at the last possible moment short of freedom.

Tilbury Jenkins' final part in the drama he had accepted reluctantly. To fire a shot, even from a well-hidden position, was risky, but it had been clear that only so drastic a measure would stop Javits from making damaging disclosures.

A bullet seemed a poor reward for services rendered, but Tilbury reminded himself that the fellow had already sold out his employer, whose own neck was in jeopardy. Since Javits' usefulness had been at an end, a bullet was also cheaper than the considerable fee he'd promised him.

It might be called the practice of economy, and certainly he had to watch his money. This entire venture, in which the possession of Randolph Ranch was the stake, was proving far more costly than he'd counted on. But once embarked upon such a course, there was no stopping or turning back.

Watching as the unconscious horseman was revived, a nasty suspicion came to lodge among his other unpleasant thoughts, and was confirmed when the covering whiskers were removed. Tilbury swore under his breath. Certainly he hadn't wanted Minifee arrested—not at this juncture; but the realization that it was Texas and not her father made it worse.

For the man now ministering to her and undoubtedly winning her gratitude was almost certainly Dan Rather.

Tilbury Jenkins had been at pains and considerable expense to acquaint himself with as many pertinent facts as possible. These included a description of Dan Rather, who had somehow blundered into the affair along the lower course of the big river, and had persisted in remaining in the thick of it ever since.

Dan Rather was half myth, half man, but probably solid enough flesh to yield mortally to a bullet properly placed. Nervously Tilbury fingered his weapon. Just one more bullet, aimed as well as the one which had silenced Javits, could certainly solve a lot of problems.

Reluctantly, he abandoned the notion. The risk was too great. It would be like Texas to pursue hotly, and she might catch a glimpse of him. Other people might hear the shot. Jealously he watched as Dan and Texas went on; then, for a third time, he headed homeward. At this meeting of the principals, questions would be asked and answers given. And those, in turn, would lead to predictable moves.

Tilbury Jenkins had long prided himself on his ability as a checker player. A man who understood the game could plan ahead, and when the time was opportune, be in a position to slaughter the opposition.

*   *   *

The sun was setting, making a splash of gold against the darkening edges of what looked like a huge cantaloupe—a proper Texas melon. Having witnessed similar scenic productions many times before, Sandy Blair was not impressed. It reminded him that it was time to eat. But here he was, out in the middle of a country almost too big to ride over, without provisions, lacking even the wages he had been promised and to which he was entitled.

Until then, his mood had been despondent. Now, tormented by hunger, it verged on anger.

Certainly it wasn't his fault that the searchers had failed to find the pardon which

Dan Rather was supposed to carry. If anyone was to be blamed, it should be Shorty Landrum who, as usual, had promoted himself to leadership and, as usual, had messed things up. All that *he'd* done was hasten to make a report to their employer, in the belief that Tilbury Jenkins should know of such things as soon as possible. And by way of thanks, he'd been fired!

He dismounted, looking about hopefully. The reminder of a slice of melon had really made him hungry. There should be something edible somewhere—a grouse or rabbit, a deer or even a cow. Any of them would make a meal. But there was nothing. Within minutes now it would be dark, which meant that the night would have to pass supperless—unless, by some chance, there might be some supplies in the saddle bags. Since this was not his horse or his saddle, he hadn't thought to look inside them. The chance was remote, but it would do no harm to look.

He searched eagerly, then pawed through in growing disgust. Just as he'd feared, there was nothing—nothing except an old, wadded-up bandana, and in the opposite bag, some paper. He was about to fling those aside in contempt when a notion hit him. Straining his eyes in the gloom, he looked more closely, and elation replaced his disgruntlement.

So this was the answer, the way in which

Dan Rather had flummoxed them, even while they held him at gun point. Somehow, with his back to the horse, he'd managed to transfer the papers to the saddle bag, hoping, of course, to recover them before the ruse could be discovered. Only his own impetuous action in taking the nearest horse and riding had spoiled that.

Here was the pardon, and its possession meant power. Men had died already battling for it, and a lot of people would pay well to obtain it.

Especially Tilbury Jenkins, who had conceived the plan in the first place. Blair, over a period of time, had pretty well pieced together the story. Jenkins coveted both Randolph Ranch and the pretty daughter of the owner, and being a man as devious as he was lacking in scruple, he'd planned elaborately, to get what he wanted.

During the war years, riding as a raider, sometimes striking far afield, Tilbury Jenkins had made acquaintances among many different sorts of men. Some of them were birds of a feather. Tilbury had enlisted support for his venture, with John Marston his most notable recruit. It was a gamble, but the stakes were huge, and when men's lives were already on the board, few boggled either at principle or penalty.

From the snatches of tales which Blair had heard, the scheme had more than once teetered on the brink of disaster. Despite that, Tilbury Jenkins had succeeded, up to this last, vital step. Now, if he held the pardon, he could dictate his own terms. Randolph Ranch, Randolph Minifee and Texas would be pawns in the game.

Jenkins had come close—closer even than he knew. Then, in his rage, he'd overstepped himself. Blair smiled crookedly. As an employee, taking good pay for lazy work, he'd been obligated to serve his employer's interests. But after being fired without cause, even without the pay due him, such obligations were erased.

Gone was his indecision. He pocketed the papers and swung back to the saddle. Supper might be delayed, but at least it wouldn't be half-roasted rabbit, without salt. When he ate, it would be in town, and high on the hog! And tomorrow—

About then, Tilbury, I'm afraid you'll be losing *your* appetite! He grinned. For wherever you eat, I'll be gnawing right along with you! This time, *I'm* crackin' the whip!

It was evening when Dan rode away from the big house on Randolph Ranch, shaking his head in an effort to clear it of notions too wild for a grown man to entertain. Randolph Minifee's welcome, as well as Texas', had been cordial, far more so than the circumstances justified. Unless and until he recovered the pardon, he deserved only their scorn.

After an initial remark or so in passing, they had said little about Tilbury Jenkins, and such reticence was as revealing as a flood of denunciation. So now his destination, under cover of the night, was Tilbury's spread, the Diamond J, more commonly termed the Fishhook.

A conglomeration of shanties and hovels appeared to huddle together as he approached, an unsavory jumble which the darkness strove to cover, but which carried its own warning on the wind. Only a couple of lights struggled against the prevailing gloom. One of these came from the house, standing somewhat aloof. A coal-oil lamp smoked on a rickety table.

The other light shone from what served apparently as a bunkhouse. It was a lantern, showing through an unshaded window. All else was dark. Dan, dismounting, moved gingerly, anticipating a rush of hounds, but there were none.

He reached the barn, resting a hand against the warped, unpainted boards, then moved on to a door hanging askew, held by a loose iron hinge at the bottom and an equally indecisive leather one near the top. Inside, there was no sound, no stirring of restless animals. The gloom was lightened by a diffusion of moonlight, filtering through a windowless opening high above.

With eyes accustomed to the murk, he found a row of saddles, hanging by stirrups from pegs on the wall. None of them was encumbered by saddle bags. Another, dumped in a corner, gave him a moment of hope. It did have the necessary adjunct, but the bags were smaller, different in pattern from the ones he sought.

When he let himself back out, he was certain that the saddle he sought was not inside. Yet · if not there, where? The possibilities were as big as Texas.

Lazy or careless punchers often slung saddles along the top bar of a corral. It was worth a look.

Hope arose as he made out three saddles, perched like hens on a roost. As he examined them, his expectations faded. None carried saddle bags. As he turned from the last, he saw the gun.

It was a shotgun, double-barreled, showing huge in the half-light. Tilbury Jenkins' voice was hoarse with eagerness.

'Grab a star, feller, and let's have a look at you. And maybe you can explain why you're prowlin'.'

A man might occasionally risk a pistol or even a six-gun, but a shotgun stuffed with buckshot was a sure ticket to Boothill. Dan obeyed both orders.

'Somebody traded saddles with me, likely by mistake, in town last night. A man riding a

142

Fishhook cayuse. I was sort of checking to see if mine was here.'

'Oh, yeah?' Triumph ran as thick and strong as black-strap molasses in Jenkins' voice. He'd left the house, intending to head for town, and it had been by luck he'd glimpsed the shadowy figure by the corral. On a hunch, he'd ducked back for the scattergun. Here was even greater luck, for he was now certain of his captive.

'That's kind of a fishy-soundin' yarn, feller,' he said contemptuously. 'If a mistake was made, seems like an honest man would come to the house and explain.'

What he suggested was both reasonable and logical. Dan was saved the need for further invention as Jenkins went on.

'I reckon that what you were really lookin' for is a pair of saddle bags—and I won't deny that it'd pleasure me if you'd found them, Dan Rather. With me watchin' you, that is.'

His words were a confession that the pardon had not been found, as well as an indication that he knew its hiding place. How he had made the discovery was not important. Dan remained silent, but any hope that his captor might make a wrong move was quickly dispelled. Jenkins kept back out of reach of any possible countermove. He, too, was an old hand at dangerous games.

'It just occurred to me that you might decide to pay us a visit, Dan Rather.' He

143

chuckled. 'You've got a reputation for doing crazy things, but this time you tried them on the wrong man. Fact is, your mistake was in decidin' to come to Texas in the first place. It's a big place—but right now it's by way of being crowded.'

Again, Dan made no reply. Usually you could pretty well size a man up merely by listening to him.

'Head across to the bunkhouse, where there's a light,' Tilbury added. 'And keep those paws up where I can see them. I have an itchy trigger finger.'

Again, Dan obeyed. Whatever his usual propensities, he had a strong feeling that this time Tilbury Jenkins was telling the truth.

Tilbury shouted ahead for those inside to open the door, then gave additional and particular instructions to the crew members. Once Dan was inside, they relieved him of his guns, including his hide-out weapon. Not until his hands had been jerked behind his back and tied did Jenkins relax. Then he tossed the shotgun onto a bunk and picked up the lantern, flashing its light full in Rather's face.

'Yeah, I was right as a hound diggin' up a bone,' he said. 'You're Dan Rather, all right. The *great* Dan Rather! Take a look, boys. You won't see such a paragon more'n every other time you go to town. Why, he even wears boots and britches, just like the rest of

144

us! Might even drink whiskey and chew on a beef bone. And was he to be stuck with a bowie, I bet he'd bleed!' He drew a slow breath, his face twisting in triumph. 'You got anything to say for yourself, Mr. Rather?'

'Right now, I'm fresh out of things to say,' Dan admitted.

'For once, I shouldn't wonder if you was likely tellin' the truth. But maybe we'll have some things to say to each other later on. Depends on how useful you turn out to be. Was I in your boots, I'd give some thought to how to be entertainin' and informative. For it runs in my mind that—otherwise—that Yankee captain might be sort of pleased to get *his* hands on you—for a variety of reasons, some of them mean and sharp.'

Dan listened attentively. So he knew about the events of the day, including the hornets! Tilbury Jenkins did not look impressive, but some of the happenings of recent weeks were at last beginning to fit into place.

'Right now I'll ride to town and have a talk with the cap'n,' Jenkins added. 'You boys entertain our guest till I either get back, or send for him—and I'd sure find it disappointin' if he wasn't to be found when I wanted him. Yes, sir, that could be disappointin' in a way that some folks maybe wouldn't enjoy.'

CHAPTER SIXTEEN

Tilbury Jenkins made his usual oblique approach, riding into town from a side road, tying his horse and moving from shadow to patch of shade like a vaguely unhappy spider traveling across its web. Finally, as though by chance, he sidled up to Rab Culdeen, as the captain emerged from the building which was being used by the soldiers as a temporary barracks.

Save for a discolored blotch on his cheek, Culdeen showed no effect of the stings. But it was common knowledge that several of his men were still unfit for duty. Jenkins surprised him by saluting, somewhat sloppily. Culdeen regarded him suspiciously. 'What's that for?'

Tilbury grinned. 'Just a sort of token, as you might say. I was thinkin' you'd earned it—duty under fire, again as you might say. Trouble can sure come at a man unexpected, can't it? Fairly arms, sometimes.'

Culdeen regarded him with disfavor, which he was at no particular pains to hide.

'I find trouble less obnoxious when it is direct,' he observed.

'Yeah, I reckon so.' Tilbury sobered. 'Now, don't misunderstand me, Cap'n. I sympathize with you. And to prove it, I'd like

146

to buy you a drink.'

Since most of his men were too ill to do anything, Culdeen was temporarily forced to curtail his activities. He shrugged and consented.

'I suppose I could drink with a Greek,' he admitted acidly.

To his surprise, Tilbury understood the allusion, and laughed instead of taking offense.

'Watch out for Greeks with a skunk in a sack, eh?' He chuckled. 'I don't blame you, Cap'n, and you're dead right. I do want something—and I figure you do, too. Maybe we can work together. My name's Jenkins—Tilbury Jenkins.'

Culdeen took careful note of that. Jenkins was some sort of a relative to Randolph Minifee. They retired to a table with their drinks. 'Well?' Culdeen prompted.

'You're in this country to catch a bird named Minifee,' Tilbury said. 'Might be we could work together there, too—a little later. Depends. Right now, your try sort of got you a bloody nose, so it occurred to me that you might like to settle—temporarily—for the man who turned those bees loose on you?'

Culdeen studied him with a growing perplexity.

'Are you suggesting that they're not one and the same man?'

Tilbury drained his own glass, then refilled

both from the bottle.

'Fooled you, did they? I don't wonder. But I happened to be at a spot where I saw what happened. Had a good view, without being in range myself, as you might say. The feller you was chasing didn't fire that bullet. Fact is, right afterward, one or two of them naturally aggravated little insects got to his horse—in a manner of speakin'—and troubled it, too. So that he got throwed, too—in a manner of speakin', again.'

'Exactly what do you mean by "a manner of speaking?"'

'Just that it wasn't him—the general—you was chasing. It was a lady—the general's daughter, wearin' a set of false whiskers. Poor gal took quite a spill, too.'

Culdeen looked startled. He had seen Texas Minifee on two or three occasions, and had been impressed, wishing dismally that he was not a Yankee, and particularly not on a Yankee mission to arrest her father.

'I didn't know that,' he confessed. 'I'm sorry—about her taking a spill, I mean.'

'I doubt she'd appreciate your sympathy. Anyway, I guess it didn't hurt her too much. The feller that fired the shot circled around to help her out. Later I picked him up, in case you're interested.'

'I'm afraid that what he did hardly comes under the heading of a crime for which he could be punished.'

'Likely not. But I take it that in the course of the war—and since—you've heard of Dan Rather?'

'Old Dan Rather? Major Rather—'

'One and the same. Used to pester you Yanks considerable, and hasn't gotten over the habit. He turned those hornets loose on you.'

Rab Culdeen looked stunned. 'I had no idea that Dan Rather was even in Texas,' he confessed.

'You have now,' Tilbury assured him comfortably. 'Do we make a deal, or not?'

Culdeen eyed his companion distastefully. Then, because he was a practical man, with a job to do, he nodded. 'Likely we can,' he conceded.

Offhand, Dan could recall no more uncomfortable twenty-four hours than the last ones had turned out to be. During the war years he had experienced many unpleasant hours, but Jenkins' crew, heeding their employer's implied threat, had gone to extreme lengths to make sure that this prisoner did not escape. Most of the time he'd lain, trussed hand and foot, barely able to wiggle. Apparently they credited Dan Rather with the ability to perform feats of legerdemain.

When at length word came to bring him into town, they still took precautions. He was untied and fed, giving his cramped limbs a chance to return partially to normal; then he was hoisted onto a horse. A strip of rawhide was looped about one foot, passed beneath the horse and tied to his other foot. His hands were tied at the wrists, this time in front of him; the purpose of that was to confine them beside the horn of the saddle with a length of wire. It was twisted about the horn, then looped over the thong between his wrists.

Three guards rode with him, one leading his horse, another riding ahead, the third behind. Even Jenkins could hardly have accused them of negligence.

Dan was thoroughly tired of captivity, and in any case, time might be running out. The odds were discouraging, but he'd faced worse and was still alive. A wind had sprung up with the dusk, following a day of calm and torpid heat. It increased in intensity, welcome only in that it stirred the air, for its buffetings were unpleasant. The man who brought up the rear made conversation, as though to allay a growing nervousness by the sound of human voices.

'Not a very nice evenin' for a ride,' he observed, glancing to where clouds scudded across the ragged sky. 'But you better enjoy it while you can, Dan Rather. Might be it's the last ride you'll be takin' for a long, long while.'

His suggestion was a perfect opening for what he had in mind. Dan nodded agreement.

'Yeah, one never knows what's going to happen next,' he conceded. 'Man is born to trouble, they say—and I'd agree with that. A night like this—why, we'll any of us be lucky if we reach the end of it.'

'What do you mean—lucky?' A thread of nervousness tore raggedly through the other's voice.

'I don't like nights like this—or weather like this,' Dan confessed, and the uneasiness in his own voice seemed almost to bubble. 'If it ends up in a twister—and we happen to be caught right in the middle—'

He paused, then went on, as though impelled by morbid memories.

'I remember one time—it was right smack about the middle of the war, and we'd been campaigning sort of off by ourselves, and we got caught smack-dab in the middle of twister country—'

He talked on and on, a fearsome, almost gruesome recital, pleased at his own inventiveness. The other three listened, fascinated, repelled, but too curious to protest. They were increasingly jittery, and jumpy nerves might prove an asset before the ride was over. For he didn't intend to be taken into town like a trussed fowl.

The thickening night, along with the dust stirred by the wind, were favorable for his attempt. To his surprise, they had left his spurs on his boots, and spurs could serve many uses. It took some working around, in the course of which his horse became increasingly jumpy, but finally he managed to catch the thong which fastened his feet, twisting the spur in it.

Once he had a hold, it required only a savage, twisting wrench to snap the thong. That again impelled the horse to pitch, but in the gloom, listening to the climax of his fearsome tale, the guards failed to notice.

Once his legs were free, the next move was difficult, but possible. For most of the ride he had been busy with his fingers, trying to twist loose the wire which anchored his hands beside the saddle-horn. Reluctantly he had reached the conclusion that it couldn't be managed. The wire was much too stiff for the limited purchase which he could exert with fingers alone.

The darkness was thick enough to conceal what he was doing, and the increasing dust accounted for any nervous movements of the cayuse. He managed to lift a leg, bringing his foot up beside the horn. Maintaining his balance was precarious, but his anchored hands helped.

Patiently he maneuvered to hook the wheel of the spur into the wire. The barbs raked his wrist, and a lurch as the horse broke from a trot to a gallop made it no easier. Then the spur caught. A quick side-twist was enough, and the wire snapped.

His wrists, free now from the saddle-horn, were still tied together, but he could make some movement. The weather was cooperating, as though to bear out his direst predictions. The wind veered, and gusts of rain spattered, although not enough to lay the dust. It swept around them in a dervish dance, blinding and choking. The horses crowded together as they ran, and this was the chance he'd played for.

Standing in the stirrups, Rather flung himself at the man beside him. In the dark it was chancy business, since a miscalculation would send him under the hoofs.

His arms looped over the guard's head and down about his shoulders. The horses veered apart, and Dan was out of the saddle, dragging his captive with him. A second man shouted, becoming aware that something was wrong, but still uncertain what was happening.

They rolled together, but luck brought him uppermost. The wind went out of his victim in a jarring whoosh; then he sprawled limply.

His revolver was half out of the holster, its butt conveniently at hand. Dan brought it up in a two-handed gesture as he rose, pointing into the face of the rear-riding guard as he jumped hurriedly from his horse.

'I'm glad to see you,' Dan assured him. 'Cut me loose—or would I be compelled to ready you for buryin', now?'

Gun or man, perhaps both, were convincing. The blade of a bowie touched lightly as a vagrant kiss upon the thong, and that was enough. Then outrider swept back, clearing his eyes of dust as the whirlwind danced away. He emptied his gun in a vicious swirl of sound, but his mistake was double. Haste spoiled his aim, while the lance of fire targeted him in turn. Dan Rather did not miss.

CHAPTER SEVENTEEN

The deal required some haggling, a procedure to which Rab Culdeen was averse, but which Tilbury Jenkins enjoyed and persisted in. Following days of apprehension, matters were again breaking right, and he intended to savor his triumph to the full.

A part of that could come when he turned Dan Rather over to the army; afterward, there was still bigger game which the boys in blue were eager to bag. What he did there would depend on Texas. He'd enjoy ridding himself of the general, since he could never be the big man in the community as long as Minifee remained. On the other hand, it would be a triumph to flash the pardon in the eyes of this Yankee captain and deny him his victim almost in the moment of victory.

Most of all, he'd enjoy forcing Randolph Minifee and his daughter to bow to his terms.

He could not forbear a slight swagger as he went on down the street. At any moment now, his men should be arriving with Dan Rather; even more pleasing, a horseman was stopping at the livery barn, revealed briefly but clearly in the light of a lantern. It was the one man he wanted to see above all others: Sandy Blair.

Jenkins was momentarily uneasy. Blair might have returned for any of a number of reasons, but there was the possibility that he had found the pardon. If that had happened, he might be difficult to handle.

Having stabled his horse, the cowboy was just starting down the street when his former employer accosted him.

'Evenin', Sandy.'

The tone was mild, but Blair knew the callous indifference which gave this man his calmness. He swung warily, prudently putting his back to the wall of the nearest building. A smile twisted his lips, but in the gloom it did not show.

'Why, evenin', Tilbury,' he returned, and waited.

Despite himself, eagerness threaded Jenkins' voice.

'I'm sure glad to see you again, Sandy. After you left, I got to thinkin', and I decided

I'd been wrong, getting mad at you the way I did. I was upset, but it wasn't your fault. After talkin' to the other boys, I made sure of that. So you can have your job back, same as before.'

'Same as ever, eh?' Blair's momentary nervousness had departed. Almost daintily, he lifted a sack of the makings from his shirt pocket, taking his time about rolling a quirly in the reflected light from the lantern at the stable door. 'Why, now, that's nice of you, Tilbury—mighty nice!'

Jenkins stiffened. Never before had Sandy or any of the hands presumed to address him by his first name. He took pains to impress upon all and sundry that he was kin to the general; therefore undue familiarity was not permissible. The sardonic note in Blair's voice was disturbing.

'I aim to be fair when I make a mistake,' he said stiffly.

'Oh, so you made a mistake, eh? Well now, maybe you did, Tilbury—maybe you did.' Blaire stuck the cigarette between his lips, unlighted.

'What do you mean, maybe I did?' Jenkins demanded suspiciously. 'I've told you I aim to do the right thing, giving you your old job back. What more do you want?'

He'd half expected the answer; still it hit him like mud in the face.

'I might want quite a lot more—the same as

you. I found what was in those saddle bags, Tilbury. And I guess you've figured out what was in them, too. That's the only thing that would account for you back-trackin' the way you're doing.'

'You mean that you found the pardon?' Tilbury asked hoarsely.

'That's sure enough what I brought to light. Havin' it, I decided I'd come back this way. Possessin' certain things makes a difference in a man's thinking.'

Jenkins digested that statement, and the threat was too clear to be misunderstood.

'I'm sure glad you found it,' he said. 'It does make a difference. Course, that was what I hired you for—to get it. But I always know how to reward loyalty.'

'Yeah—by firing a man without a reason,' Blair reminded him dryly.

'Uh—I told you I make a mistake. I'll give you a good bonus for what you've done.'

'You sure will, Tilbury. I've got the pardon now—and I know what it's worth. And after the way you fired me without no reason, I don't owe you a thing—certainly not from loyalty.'

'All right.' Jenkins swallowed painfully and capitulated. 'How much do you want?'

'Well—riding in this way, I had plenty of time to think. You like to brag about being kin to the general, but I don't recollect ever hearing *him* mention anything about being

157

kin to you. So maybe he ain't so proud of it. And there's a couple of other points. He's got a lot more land and cattle than you have. And it's his life that's at stake.'

'Are you tryin' to suggest that I would think of money ahead of the gen'ral's life?' Tilbury tried to sound horrified.

'I know perfectly well that it's what you're thinking about,' Blair informed him callously. 'You'd sell your own mother if you saw your way to a profit. Right now, I've something to sell. Do you figure you can pay a better price than the general?'

This was worse than he'd feared—so much worse that Jenkins made the mistake of losing his temper a second time.

'You're a stinkin' Yankee if you think I'd bargain with you on such a basis,' he growled, and sounded convincingly righteous. 'I wouldn't think of going against my kin, General Minifee, where his interests are at stake. So that little scheme ain't going to work!'

The wind had blown itself away, along with most of the clouds. The moon had emerged, and in its light, Blair's shrug was easy to see.

'In that case, I'm wastin' time botherin' with you. The general ain't my kin, and I happen to know that he's on the government's list of wanted men—and that there's a Yankee captain here in town looking for him. I figure the general is fond enough of his life to pay me for my trouble. If he won't, maybe his girl will. Anyhow, I'll go find out.'

It could be a bluff, and probably was. Few men cared to confront Randolph Minifee with any proposition which smacked of the dubious. But Tilbury Jenkins was no poker player, and he distrusted those who did play.

'No, wait,' he protested. 'We got the same interests in this, and we can work things a lot better by doing them together. We—I figure we can make a deal.'

Blair turned back. His smile was contemptuous.

'In other words, when you're over a barrel, you'll squeal like any other hog,' he said bitingly. 'But there's some sense in what you say. We can work it better together. If it wasn't for that, I sure wouldn't bother with you.'

Jenkins swallowed. 'How much do you want?' he managed.

'All I can get,' Blair returned bluntly. 'You're playin' for big stakes—Randolph Ranch itself. I want half.'

'Half?' The word was an agonized bleat. 'Why, that's robbery.'

'That's what we're indulgin' in, ain't it? Robbery—with murder on the side. Take it or leave it.'

Tilbury Jenkins liked to haggle, but he could recognize when he was beaten, when argument could be not only futile but

159

dangerous. He nodded and spread his hands in token of defeat.

'All right,' he acknowledged. 'I'll take it. And now let's have that pardon. The sooner we get this done, the better.'

'I agree with you there. But you don't think I'd be fool enough to carry it on me, do you—knowing you?'

Tilbury's fingers had been itching for his gun, balancing the risk against the rewards. He smothered a sigh.

'I ain't one to cut off my nose to spite my face,' he protested. 'Do this any way you like, only let's be about it.'

The only trouble, when they returned to the stable and examined the saddle bags, which Blair had again selected as a temporary hiding place, was that they were empty.

Jenkins swung on Blair in a fury. 'If you're tryin' to play games with me—' he blazed.

The bewilderment on Blair's was too plain to be faked, and Jenkins paused, but only for a moment.

'Once you had your hands on that paper, you should have known enough to keep hold of it,' he raved. 'Only a fool would go and lose it again this way.'

He broke off, considering. Who could have taken the pardon this time? Its very existence was supposedly a well-kept secret. Dismally, against reason, he had a conviction that when the answer came, it would have the name of

Dan Rather stamped upon it.

When circumstances required, Dan Rather could present a rough façade to the world, as he had when making the challenge of triple Russian roulette. Ordinarily he preferred to move without the sound of trumpets. He reached the town, skirting the square and its mild activity, and approached the livery barn from the darkest shadows. He had allowed his ex-guards to go their own way, with only the mild suggestion that he would rather not encounter then again too soon.

'You won't, Major—not if we can help it,' one of them had promised fervently, while the other gave full concurrence. 'Me, I've just remembered some urgent business down Santone way—and it'd be a shame to keep anybody waitin'!'

Still in the shadows, Dan dismounted. The big doors of the barn stood wide to the summer night, and the interior yawned cavernously, its spaciousness emphasized by the small glow of a single lantern, hung from a cross-beam just inside the door. Outlined in the radiance, a man moved. Recognizing him, Dan sucked in his breath, keeping the sound soft, and fingered the gun which again filled his holster.

Sandy Blair moved as far as the doorway, then turned back. He crossed to where a saddle rested, opened the flap of a pair of saddle bags, and transferred something from his pocket to the container. That done, he left the stable, moving with brisk assurance.

His departure was checked by a hail from Tilbury Jenkins. Dan listened with interest to the heated warmth of their greetings, then edged around to a side door and let himself into the barn. It was filled with the sounds of occupancy—horses who shifted position, chewed contentedly or sighed as they settled themselves for the night. The saddle was deep among the shadows.

He recognized it by the intricately carved leatherwork, and the saddle bags were the ones he sought. Retrieving the packet placed there by Blair, he slipped outside again, waiting until the others had looked and departed, quarreling.

He was desperately tired. The previous night, like the day, had been anything but restful. Now that the pair had gone, he saw no reason to look further. As he led his horse inside, a man materialized from the gloom of a side room which served as an office. Unlike the slovenly, straw-chewing individual who had earlier served that function, he moved with military precision and erectness, though the effect was somewhat spoiled by a noticeable limp.

'Good evenin', suh,' he observed, then stopped, staring. His face, long and blue-jowled from the closeness of a recent shave, went blank with surprise. The look was as swiftly replaced by pleased recognition. One hand flew up in salute.

'Major Rather, suh, I'm right happy to see you again,' he declared.

Dan stared in equal surprise, then thrust out his hand.

'Sergeant Tring!' he exclaimed. 'Now this is a pleasant surprise, finding you here!'

Tring hesitated, abashed. He eyed the outstretched hand, rubbed his own furtively along his trousers, then accepted the handshake with a hearty grip.

'I thought I'd see something of the country, sir—havin' nothin' better to do,' he explained. 'I'll see that your horse gets the best of care, sir.'

'I'm sure you will,' Dan agreed. 'Could you manage as much for me, Tring—a chance to sleep in the hay? I'll be leaving early.'

Tring nodded imperturbably. Having ridden many times with Dan Rather on dawn forays, he had no need to ask what early might mean.

'You don't need to ask, suh. And if you say the word, suh, I'll be happy to ride with you.'

'Thanks, Sergeant, but it won't be necessary—this time.' Dan accepted the horse blanket which Tring extended in a wordless gesture and retreated to a far corner of the hayloft. There, in the dim reflected glow from the lantern, he checked the pardon again and looked longingly at the photo. He frowned,

reading again the bold line across the bottom:
'With all my love. Texas.'

Sighing, he returned both to his pocket and fell asleep.

CHAPTER EIGHTEEN

For Tilbury Jenkins, the night was not restful. He repaired to the saloon, not so much to drink as to think, doing that at a remote table, cherishing a single bottle through most of the night. He was oblivious to the disgruntled glances of the bartender, forced to keep open on his account long after other customers had departed. Jenkins was deep in a problem, and he needed to solve it at once.

Planning—some unkindly called it scheming—had always been his strong point. He could act when occasion required, but to think a problem through was of far greater importance. And gradually, as the night wore on, its untroubled peacefulness brought him the answer.

He realized with a start that the trio he'd sent for—the three who were to bring Dan Rather to town—had not reported in from the Fishhook. In his dismay at finding the pardon again strayed or lost, he had temporarily forgotten about other things. They should have reached town hours before. The fact that they had not could mean only one thing.

Somehow Dan Rather must have done it again—in this case, he had escaped from an impossible situation, and made sure that those who had been set to guard him did not report the circumstances. What might have happened to them was of no interest to Jenkins, since it was obvious that they had failed. Now the disappearance of the pardon was equally disastrous. It was again in the hands of Dan Rather.

Tilbury swore, overturning his chair and jarring the table as he came abruptly to his feet. Disregarding the startled interest of the bartender, he headed for the door and out. The answer was so obvious that he should have guessed it immediately. Instead, he'd wasted precious hours, and Dan might already be handing that damaging piece of paper over to Randolph Minifee or, even worse, placing it in the hands of Texas.

On the other hand, Rather might choose to get a night's sleep before setting out to deliver it. Tied up as he had been while an involuntary guest on Fishhook, he would certainly be in poor shape, on the verge of exhaustion. The possibility still afforded a chance, and so long as one remained, he'd play the game to a conclusion.

Tring, remarkably wide awake for a man roused at such an early hour of the morning, brought Tilbury's horse at his request, asking no questions. He saw no reason to explain that he had been awakened, only minutes earlier, as Dan Rather had saddled his own horse and took off. That was strictly the major's business.

Tilbury Jenkins, burning with impatience, paused as Blair came hurrying, attracted by the commotion. 'I'll ride with you,' he said briefly. Chafing, Tilbury acceded, since acquiescence was easier than argument. It was Blair, as they spurred out of town, who sniffed the night air and wrinkled his nose like a hound catching a fresh scent.

'Dust,' he observed tersely. 'Somebody's been stirring it up just ahead of us. Ain't hardly had time to settle.'

A faint haze was undeniable in the air. The cause had escaped Tilbury, but he nodded grudgingly, swinging to look moodily toward the south. Off in that direction there was also a stir of activity, despite the early hour. Off there was the barracks, occupied now by the Yankee soldiers. What was Culdeen up to?

'You never can tell about those blasted Yankees,' he growled, and his horse leaped to the goad of the spurs.

At least they were ahead of the army, if they were also heading this way; also, the dust was stronger, an indication that they were gaining on whoever had stirred it. The sky tonight was cloudless, a field of purple blue sprinkled by a million stars. In their midst, the moon swam serenely. The combined efforts of stars and moon gave only a passable light, but with eyes accustomed to the gloom, both horsemen made out the lone rider ahead, a man who rode at a steady, unhurried trot.

Again, it was Blair who made the identification.

'That's Dan Rather,' he pronounced, and flicked a sharply calculating glance at his companion. 'You figured that it would be?'

Jenkins satisfied himself that it was indeed Dan Rather who rode ahead. The night had not been wasted, after all. He nodded.

'Yeah,' he conceded. 'I thought it might be.'

Blair was not long in arriving at the obvious.

'And he's got the pardon back, of course!'

'Seems likely, don't it?'

'Guess it does.' Unwilling admiration was in Blair's voice. For a few hours, he had enjoyed a feeling of superiority. Now he was forced to concede that, however unprepossessing in looks and manner Tilbury might be, the man was smarter than he appeared.

Jenkins took no notice of the admiration. He was busy with a new notion, discarding it as it popped into his mind, then bringing it back as a cow does her cud, liking it better as he chewed it over. Of course it was risky, even dangerous. On the other hand, the possible rewards were tempting.

Nor was it as though he had never done that sort of thing before. His training as a guerilla had long since cured him of squeamishness when it came to the shedding of another's blood. One more on the list was nothing to boggle about.

Last evening, he'd consented to Blair's demands, which had amounted to virtual blackmail, agreeing only because he'd had no choice. But Blair had bungled, as all his underlings seemed to do, and that failure had cancelled the pact. It was his own planning which had brought him on the trail of Dan Rather at this hour, along a lonely road, and he needed no help with the job. Also, if Blair thought that he was going to cut himself in again for a full partnership—

'How will we work this?' Blair asked. 'Kill him or catch him?'

The question suggested the answer he'd been looking for. Despite the thread of admiration in Blair's voice, his eager willingness to cooperate, Tilbury took note of the part that his companion continued to watch him like a hawk. If ever the cowboy had had any illusions concerning his employer, recent events had dissipated them. He appeared to entertain precisely the amount of trust for Tilbury Jenkins that he would have accorded a coiled rattlesnake.

'I'd like to kill him,' Tilbury admitted viciously. 'But that's risky—and he may be worth more to us alive. He don't guess that he's being followed yet. And those Yankees will pay a bounty for him—alive. One of us can circle, get ahead and cut him off.'

Blair nodded. He'd been thinking along the same lines.

'I'll cut around,' he agreed, and set his horse to a faster pace, swinging at an angle. Jenkins watched, smiling grimly. This would require fast and well-timed action, but he had no doubt as to his ability. Most of his fighting during the war years had been by starlight. Some activities were better handled under cover of darkness.

A rifle was slung in a sheath beside the saddle. He'd used it to make certain that Javits would hold fast his secret, re-proving its accuracy. But even should one or two bullets go wide of the target, there were others instantly ready to rectify the mistake.

The range was about right, close enough for his purpose, yet with space between should anything go wrong. Dan Rather's horse was slowing to a walk as it climbed a slope. Apparently he had no suspicion that he was being followed. Blair was about an equal distance, off at one side.

Scrub oaks formed a convenient cover from which to operate. From beneath such a screen, a killer would be impossible to identify.

He pulled up and dismounted. He prided himself on his marksmanship, even fron a running horse, but most cayuses disliked having a gun blasting above their ears; a jerk of the head at the wrong instant could spoil an aim. And tonight he couldn't afford to miss.

From there, also, the angle was right. Those who later bothered to investigate would see that a bullet might as easily have been fired from where Dan Rather traveled as from that far back along the trail. It was only a trifling thing, but careful attention to small details had a way of paying off.

Jenkins swung the gun up, fitting the stock against his shoulder. Momentarily he hesitated, at a loss which target to take first. Dan Rather was more important than the cowboy, who had suddenly grown too big for his boots. But it was Blair who had dared to threaten him, presuming to make demands on the man who was kin to the general! That sort of conduct was unpardonable.

Actually, the order of precedence didn't matter. He could fire two shots in as many seconds, and two would be enough. Jenkins lined his victim in the sights, and his finger curled about the trigger.

The thrust of the stock against his shoulder was satisfying, as was the result, instantly visible. Even at that distance, he could see

Blair start to spill from the saddle. He spared a second to make sure, then swung the muzzle of the rifle toward the other rider.

Incredulously, with hands suddenly sweaty, he stared. The gun muzzle bobbed. Once again, Dan Rather had disappeared.

CHAPTER NINETEEN

Tilbury blinked in disbelief. It simply was not possible, not even for a man whose feats had become legendary. Then he understood, and disgust for his own stupidity vied with rage. It was a trick of the light, coupled with the terrain, but he knew every foot of the country and should have been alerted.

Dan Rather did not reappear. At the spot where he had been riding, the road made a sudden dip, dropping out of sight. Then the trail came back into sight. But, warned by the sound of the gun, Dan Rather did not. He'd be circling in turn, trying to catch a glimpse of the killer.

Blair's horse had stopped as the reins fell from a nerveless hand. There was no longer any reason for it to run. But there might be for others. Tilbury Jenkins lost no time in seeking deeper cover.

Dan Rather rode steadily, and it was habit as much as anything else which caused him to veer away from the road as soon as he was out of town. It was time to face reality, to set his thoughts and emotions in order.

Once again he'd acted like a moon-struck youth, taking out the photo and studying it as he rode, finally replacing it in his pocket with a sigh. Moon or no moon, it was worse than moon-madness to dream. That message, written across the bottom of the photograph, was not and never had been for him.

The crash of the rifle jarred him, and instantly he was alert. From where he rode he could not see where the shot had come from, but he did see the victim. The light was poor, but there was something familiar about the man spilling from the saddle. It looked like Blair.

Once he knew that much, the rest was easy to guess. Blair worked for Tilbury Jenkins, so he must have been riding to cut Dan off. In the midst of that operation he had been stopped by a bullet as unexpected as it was murderous.

The reason for such a shot was not inexplicable. Blair had become an ally rather than an employee, and in that he played a dangerous game.

Probably the killer had planned to kill both of them, but the dip in the trail had come at an opportune moment for Dan. Which meant that Tilbury would be after him, more desperate and determined than ever.

Distant shouts broke the silence. Other men were abroad despite the hour, horsemen probably as disturbed as they were puzzled by what had just occurred. Through the trees, Dan caught a glimpse of the uniforms and understood. Captain Rab Culdeen was also planning an early morning call at Randolph Ranch.

The buildings were not far ahead, and the early dawn was even closer. Moon and stars paled as a glow flushed the east; then the avenue of trees blazed in the first touch of the sun.

Cowboys, like farmers, are notoriously early risers. Already, disregarding the clock, the cook was about his duties, a finger of smoke testing the air above the cook shack, the clatter of pans ringing far in the stillness. Two or three men moved near the barn, walking as though not yet fully awake or adjusted to the demands of the new day.

From there on, there was no cover except the avenue, unless one circled to approach the buildings from the north or west. It was a choice of following between the trees or along either side. Both sources left a man clearly visible. Dan swung between.

The flash of sun on a lifting rifle barrel warned him, even as Jenkins' voice rapped out. Tilbury crouched behind a tree, almost completely sheltered.

'Stop and hand it over, Rather—or chew a

bullet. I don't much care which!'

The last part of the statement was not entirely correct. His personal inclination was to kill this man, for vengeance would be sweet. But possession of the pardon was more important, and his chances of obtaining it would be improved if shooting could be avoided.

In the last analysis, the choice was Dan Rather's. Tilbury Jenkins had the drop, and at that distance he couldn't miss.

Dan estimated his chances and came to the same conclusion. He wasn't too surprised that Jenkins had gotten ahead of him, after being behind. As Texas had demonstrated so well on her ride, knowledge of the country made a big difference. There were trails through the brush, short cuts that a stranger would not even guess at.

To try and reach his gun would invite a bullet. Even if he had it in hand, there was no target to shoot at.

'I'm waitin',' Tilbury warned, 'but not for long!'

Here was the devil of a mess, he thought angrily. He'd been willing to show his hand enough to get what he wanted, but all his planning had envisaged himself as remaining aloof and in the background. He was the kinsman of the general, therefore a man above petty affairs. And once he was the squire of Randolph Ranch, there were few who would have the temerity even to whisper what they thought, let alone say it aloud.

Now he was forced into the open, a bandit as surely as he had been during the war years; and this time, even if he became boss of the big ranch, he would never be able to live it down. Well, the devil with it, as long as he got what he wanted—

He blenched, and for an instant the gun muzzle described a jiggling arc. There had seemed to be trouble enough, but here was the capstone. Texas was riding toward them, coming at a fast run down the avenue.

She rode a white horse, and her uncovered hair was flying in the breeze. Excitement had set battle flags in her cheeks. Never had she looked lovelier, more desirable, or more unattainable. In that moment it came to Tilbury that he had lost, no matter what might otherwise be achieved.

His snarl was urgent.

'Hand it over—or I'll kill you, right in front of her!'

Dan had no doubt that he meant it. Jenkins had schemed on a grand scale, the stake an empire. The plan had been months in the making, and men had died because of it. Frustration served only to increase Jenkins' rage. With nothing more to lose and something still to gain, he'd go as far as he had to.

Texas was coming fast, but there was still

too much time and distance between her and the men. Her face was anxious as she sensed that something was wrong, but could not be certain what it might be. The very early arrival of Dan Rather surely was significant, and the way he had stopped, to sit immobilized in the middle of the avenue, warned her that the situation must be serious. Then she understood, as Tilbury's voice lashed at her.

'Stop right there, Texas! Come any closer, and I'll blast your pretty boy right off his horse!'

Understanding, she pulled up, clapping one hand to her mouth to choke back a scream. The sun on the rifle barrel backed the threat.

'Stay put,' Tilbury added coldly. 'Try anything, and it'll mean he dies—sudden!'

Later in the day, there would be a burning heat in the sun, but at that hour of dawn, the air held a vibrant quality. At the moment, he had the drop, and with it, control. But it couldn't last. Jenkins spoke again.

'For the last time, I want that pardon! Get it out of your pocket and toss it to me—now! I'll count to three!'

He did not explain what he would do if his command was not obeyed, nor was there need. Once the pardon was in his possession, Tilbury Jenkins would know how to use it. Some of the force of his club had been weakened, but after planning so long, he would go all the way.

His eyes swiveled at a new sound, then jerked nervously back. Dan and Texas were looking, also. But he was still sheltered by the big tree, and he still had the drop.

'One,' he warned. 'Two—'

Rab Culdeen was coming down the avenue, eight men riding behind him. They would be there in a couple of minutes.

'You seem to hold the cards,' Dan Rather admitted. 'I'm getting down.'

Tilbury watched warily as he dismounted, but Dan made no move toward his gun. For that matter, he made none toward his pocket. He turned instead, his back to the gunman, and started walking toward the oncoming line of blue.

There was already some warmth in the Texas sun, but the gamble that might bring sudden death was like a chill wind in the dawn. The face of Texas had gone as white as his own, but Dan could not see.

Jenkins stared, and his jaw sagged. This was the one move he hadn't foreseen, which he could not control. This was the sort of act which had made Old Dan Rather a legend while still in his twenties.

If he fired now, shooting so brave a man in the back, he wouldn't be able to get away. He'd be gunned down in turn, or else tried for murder; and with Sandy Blair also

177

counted in the toll, he'd hang.

Tilbury watched, and grayness frosted his face. He allowed the rifle to fall, as Dan Rather took the pardon from his pocket and flourished it before the eyes of Rab Culdeen.

'Good morning, Captain,' he greeted him. 'I've something here for you to see—though I want Miss Texas Minifee to have the honor of presenting it to you! And may I add that for once I'm happy to see Yankee soldiers!'

Culdeen leaned forward to scrutinize the paper which Dan held for his perusal, but did not extend for him to grasp. Texas came up, halting beside Dan. Her eyes were shining, and the glow was brightened by tears.

Culdeen bowed as ceremoniously as the structures of the saddle would permit.

'You are Major Rather,' he observed. 'I have had the pleasure of seeing Miss Minifee before. I assure you both, I am happy to honor this pardon from our great and lamented President.'

He flushed, meeting her eyes, which held both gratitude and question, and something of a challenge. His voice turned gruff.

'I wish that I could say as much as regards you, Major. But unless you can produce a similar document in regard to yourself—as much as I dislike such duty—I shall have to take you into custody in place of General Minifee. Your name is on the same proscribed list, and I'm afraid there are those even more eager to have you laid by the heels.'

Dan nodded. 'I expected that,' he acknowledged.

Texas had the look of a small girl whose doll had been broken.

'Oh, no,' she protested. 'You can't take him—'

It was a morning of early risers, in which many horsemen seemed to be abroad. A newcomer rode briskly into sight, and Dan stared in surprise. He was given a flashing grin and a nod, but the horseman's business was with Rab Culdeen.

CHAPTER TWENTY

'I trust that you will pardon me, Captain, if I intervene to void your work,' he observed, 'though as one officer to another, I am sure that you will be happy to be relieved of such a disagreeable chore. My credentials, sir. I am Lieutenant Vanstyne, on detached special duty, as these papers explain.'

He dismounted and turned to Dan, holding out his hand.

'I am happy to see you again, sir, and to arrive, as it appears, in time to be of at least slight service. I've been driving hard ever since St. Louis, but somehow you got ahead, and I never could catch up. I am empowered to investigate special cases—such as yours—and to make recommendations. In your case, Major, I'm taking the responsibility for declaring you fully cleared of any charges resulting from the late war. I had pretty well convinced myself that the charges lodged against you were merely the result of spite when I boarded the *Mississippi Belle*. My personal observations have borne out the conclusion. I'm happy to be of even small service, after what you did for me—'

He broke off, looking to where Culdeen and some of his men were taking Tilbury Jenkins into custody. He had tried to slip away. Dan returned Vanstyne's grin. Then he borrowed a knife and carefully cut open a seam of his shirt.

'In that case, I'll restore your ring as well,' he observed. 'It has been a source of worry to me, for I've been rather thoroughly searched two or three times. I'll explain later how I came by it.'

Vanstyne's face was suddenly pale under the tan. He accepted the diamond, gulping, once again at a loss, as he had been aboard the packet on the evening when he had been mulcted of it.

'My ring,' he managed. 'Why, I—Dan, you don't know what this means to me—you can't. Entirely aside from its value, it's an heirloom, and the family honor—not to mention the Vanstyne luck—are supposed to be tied up in it. Now I never can catch up with you—though I suppose that isn't to be wondered at.'

A final actor came, galloping onto the scene; and at the sight of him, it was Dan's turn to stare with sagging jaw, while the face of Texas went white and red by turns.

During the long overland journey, Colonel John Marston had lost some of the outward appearance of a gentleman. But his aplomb remained as he flourished a battered hat and bowed to Texas.

'Good morning, Texas, my dear,' he greeted. 'I pray and trust that I am not too late. I've exerted every effort to overtake this scoundrel, who robbed me and left me for dead.'

His story was interesting, in that he was finally forced to concede that it had been Captain Hanning, of the *Belle*, who had been the cause of his detention. The bullet which had laid him low had struck a locket which he carried over his heart. The lead had flattened without penetrating, but the force of the blow, directly over his heart, had rendered him unconscious, apparently dead.

Captain Hanning had followed his own judgment. Two attempts had been made upon the colonel's life within a matter of hours, and he wanted no murder aboard his boat. To guard against a further try, he had

181

let it be inferred that the bullet had been fatal, that Marston was dead. He had assigned two men to nurse and guard the injured Marston until the packet docked at St. Louis.

Finding the pardon gone, and correctly assuming that Dan Rather might have taken it, Marston had hardly been grateful for Hanning's precautions. Now he had caught up. Texas listened to his further denunciations, and the flags were back in her cheeks.

'It seems to me, Colonel Marston, that you are speaking and acting recklessly,' she charged. 'By your own account, Major Rather had nothing to do with your detention. Instead, he had saved your life only a short while before. Believing you dead, he undertook to carry out your mission, to deliver the pardon—which he has done. Your complaints regarding him are in keeping with your past conduct—and your motives for obtaining the pardon, in the first place, were hardly as unselfish as his have turned out to be in delivering it!'

There was more. Texas Minifee, when aroused, could express herself forcefully and pointedly. Dan, his eyes matching hers in excitement, had heard enough to begin to hope that dreams could sometimes carry over into reality. Presently, after the discomfited colonel had gone elsewhere, he was emboldened to pose the question which baffled him. He drew the photograph from his pocket and held it out to Texas.

'Ever since I first set eyes on this picture, I've teetered between hope and despair, heaven and hell,' he confessed. 'Heaven when I looked at you—and your eyes in the picture looked back, as though it were meant for me! And hell, when I read what you'd written on sending the picture to him.'

Texas accepted the picture and studied it with downcast eyes, her color heightened. She smiled demurely, then, seeing the misery in Dan's face, hearing the throb in his voice, she became abruptly the woman of the picture.

'Did you wonder, Dan?' she asked. 'I suppose you would—being you. You're not like some men—such as Tilbury Jenkins or John Marston. And for that I'm thankful! That picture was stolen by Marston from my father—and what I'd written was for Dad, not for any other man—not then, at least!'

Photoset, printed and bound in Great Britain by
REDWOOD PRESS LIMITED, Melksham, Wiltshire

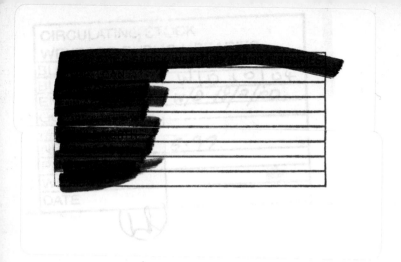

CIRCULATING STOCK